This is a work of fiction. Names, characters, businesses, places, events and incidents are either the products of the author's imagination or used in a fictitious manner. Any resemblance to actual persons, living or dead, or actual events is purely coincidental.

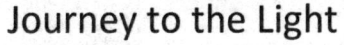

Elizabeth Elliot

Journey to the Light

Vanguard Press

VANGUARD PAPERBACK

© Copyright 2023
Elizabeth Elliot

The right of Elizabeth Elliot to be identified as author of
this work has been asserted by her in accordance with the
Copyright, Designs and Patents Act 1988.

All Rights Reserved

No reproduction, copy or transmission of this publication
may be made without written permission.
No paragraph of this publication may be reproduced,
copied or transmitted save with the written permission of the
publisher, or in accordance with the provisions
of the Copyright Act 1956 (as amended).

Any person who commits any unauthorised act in relation to
this publication may be liable to criminal
prosecution and civil claims for damages.

A CIP catalogue record for this title is
available from the British Library.

ISBN 978-1-80016-487-1

*Vanguard Press is an imprint of
Pegasus Elliot Mackenzie Publishers Ltd.*
www.pegasuspublishers.com

First Published in 2023

**Vanguard Press
Sheraton House Castle Park
Cambridge England**

Printed & Bound in Great Britain

To my children who are my world

Acknowledgements

My husband and family who supported me through this process

Chapter 1
Daily Life

It had been a long day. The light already fading to dusk. Emily gazed out of the small window in the hospital cubicle only to see the remainder of the day evaporate. She had only caught a glimpse of the light this morning on her way to work. Life, these days was mostly spent in the dark. The harsh Minnesota winter was wearing on her mood. The bleakness of the grey skies, dirty snow, and biting cold. All serve to punish the inhabitants of the frozen state. The winter reaches maximum austerity this time of year. Each day is to be survived rather than enjoyed. Emily had always felt the heavy burden of the cold more than most. She was more than a little embarrassed for this weakness. But not today. There was mounting excitement at the thought of leaving the hospital. Today she was determined to leave on time and without the usual guilt. Emily was almost buoyant at the thought. She had been a medicine/pediatric or med-peds resident for almost four years. It had been brutal, but she had learned an almost insurmountable volume of information over this time. Acquisition of medical knowledge and practical skills, such as how to soothe frustrated and tired parents, frightened patients, overworked nurses and cynical attendings, whilst making a dent in the never-ending workload. To know when the donuts were being delivered in the doctors' lounge in order to get the cream-filled treats before they vanished. To learn the peculiarities of each rotation and each attending. To know the questions that they were likely to ask on rounds and when they liked to round, the order they liked seeing patients, and how they liked debrief post-rounding. To make friends with the nurses and clerical staff. These were invaluable skills. Learning how to eat almost anything and to sleep standing up for minutes at a time were also treasured proficiencies. Emily knew this was the make it or break it time for any newly minted doctor. She was in the final stretch as a resident. The days of being impressed by a pager or trying to impress the attending or proudly wearing her white coat were long over. Hours blended one into another, no longer being separated into time of day, but merely into jobs needing to be done, pages to be answered, numbers collected, patients to be seen, orders to be signed, and notes to be charted etc. There was a time along this harsh journey of tasks, that she realized her impact and grave responsibility for life. The various tasks told a story of someone's life. Past, present and future. The 'jobs' could mean health or disease, life or death. She would have been more terrified of this fact had it not been for the utter exhaustion. Emily had already understood and respected the fragility of life. She was aware that you could be talking to a patient about their labs and overall progress and then you are pounding on their chest and bagging their failing lungs. There were many nights when Emily was haunted by the sheer tragedy. The tears when a child's life ends, the beautiful innocent life taken. A life that could not be saved. One that she had wracked her brain over, read every article, consulting service after service. Only to see the desperation and despair in the parents' eyes when their baby, their world, was gone. Emily was surprised by the mad fury that some patients, people, leave this world. Only to be contrasted with the gentleness that others perish, with the softness of a whisper. The baby with multi-organ failure who was starting to improve, but without a parent to visit or to hold her. Her damaged body and brain without the love or the protection of a mother. A mother who had relinquished her sick baby weeks ago. She just stopped visiting. The broken child left to battle this world on her own. There were countless nights after checking on other patients, when the hospital was quieter, with only the whirr of machines and the beeping of IVs finishing, Emily would hold this baby. She would talk to her and the baby would snuggle in her arms once she had transitioned to the pediatric floor from the pediatric intensive care unit, the PICU. At first, the baby would look at her blankly, but eventually she would smile and coo when she came to pick her up. Emily would look forward to this indulgence, especially amid so much chaos. Eventually this baby would be placed with foster parents. Emily had thought about taking on this task, but then realty would kick in and remind her that she did not have time for her own family, much less a medically complicated infant who would need intensive services and care. Emily currently chose five minutes extra in bed rather than combing her hair; the thought of caring for this beautiful and damaged baby was laughable. For now, she would savor holding this baby, each meeting a need in one another. Briefly connecting and then alone again amongst the bedlam.

Her own babies were given hit or miss care from their dad and the neighbor lady. Oliver was almost four and Rachel was twenty-two months. They had both been relatively unplanned. Oliver had been conceived when Emily had forgotten two birth control pills in a row when she had been taking her medical school exams. Rachel was here due to Emily being post-call and forgetting that she was no longer on the pill. She was more than a little embarrassed for her lack of planning, but thankful for both of her children. Emily was almost thirty years old; it seemed an arbitrary number. She mostly thought of her age in terms of how many months to go before finishing her residency and being able to see her children. Also, to finally get paid a living wage. Family had only been seen in parcels of time since becoming a resident. She was often so exhausted when she did see her family that she would fight sleep and her tiredness to spend some time with her children. She would routinely fall asleep in the middle of a show or story. This was a risk anytime she could sit and be quiet for more than five minutes at a time. Wanting to act like it was normal to be away from your babies for more than thirty-one hours at a time and to see your colleagues or the nursing staff more than your own family.

Emily was quickly brought back to the present upon seeing one of the nurses in the brightly lit hallway. "Mary, could you recheck vitals on Alice in forty-two A? And then Q four vitals. Thanks. Give the report to Dr Adams. I am away for the next week." Mary shook her head with affirmation of her response to the request and smiled as she knew what it meant to have time away. She was pretty, petite and energetic. Emily had come to rely her humor and good clinical judgement. Colleen the tall thin nurse on the floor tonight, who was just holding it together, as her personal life was falling apart. There were numerous stories being played out without much fanfare or notice. The day-to-day heroics that had almost become routine. Emily was humbled thinking about the people who take care of patients at the most vulnerable times of their lives. They are often white knuckling it just to make through the day. Emily would be lost in these private dramas of the hospital, and would suddenly be reminded of her children. She would see a child in clinic or on the unit in the hospital. Often it would be a toy or their feistiness which would bring a pang of regret for the time taken away from her babies.

She did not realize how profoundly she would miss her children when she started her residency. The physical ache to see and touch them. To do normal things, like going to the park or lying in with them in the morning. She had to finish the residency. She could not afford *not* to. There had been so many tests and so much money spent. So many nights of foregoing simple pleasures to be in this position, so much time. No, she would finish. She would be able to take care of her children. Her husband could never earn what she eventually would earn. She would need this income to pay off their mountain of debt. They had some money saved, but this was meagre compared to their student loans. There was no other way out of this situation. She would console herself with the fact that they were being cared for by their father, mostly. Emily was fully aware that she and Luke had made their decisions with their eyes wide open. She just did not want her children to pay for these choices. The guilt she felt when advising parents how to take care of their children to foster their best health and development, when her children were given haphazard parenting, which kept them alive and barely moving to the next milestone. She was thankful that her children had been relatively healthy, except for a few minor illnesses. She did worry about Oliver's clarity of speech and Rachel's poor impulse control, but these would need to be addressed on a calmer and more rested day. Life and death trumps all.

The privilege of her position was not lost on Emily. She only hoped she could live up to this commission, at least some of the time. She loved this part of her job. She loved her patients. Often living vicariously through them. She found it easier to relate to her patients in their defined roles, without the need for superficial small talk. Their interactions were real and about the pared down issues that mattered. Emily had little interest or patience with the world of social niceties and half-truths. She had learned what she needed to know. Her experiences had taught her to trust what was real, no matter how painful, rather than the sanitized pretentious versions of life. Her patients were mostly grateful for this fact.

Chapter 2
Family Life

Today Emily would think about something other than the lives in the hospital, a place which had become her universe. Today she would focus on her own little universe consisting of her husband and two young children. They would have seven whole days together. She had just started her month of clinic, which allowed her the break from the hospital. Her family would be leaving the frigid weather for the warm sunshine of Florida. She knew Orlando and Cocoa Beach were cliché tourist destinations, but she did not care. It was warm and cheap. She would play with her children and go to the beach. She would have margaritas outside with her husband and wake up next to each other. Compared to her current eighty-hour work week and life in the Minnesota darkness, it seemed as exotic as Bali. She would not allow herself to think about this trip as if it may somehow jinx its occurrence. Her vacation would be pulled due to a sick resident or one with a family crisis. This could happen at any time. But not now, Emily silently pleaded. Once walking out of the hospital, she started feeling a little giddy at the thought of not being there for an entire week. It would take a few more days before

Emily could bring herself to turn off her pager. Emily walked across the snowy parking lot where a soft billowy coating of white had covered the cars during the day. She could just make out her dirty green highlander at the far end of the lot, peeking out from under the mantle of snow. It had over one hundred thousand miles and was not much to look at, but always started first time. There was a stillness in the below zero temperature, which was only interrupted by the squeaking of the snow beneath Emily's boots. She haphazardly brushed off the snow from her windshield and rear window and got into her car. So far, so good. The frozen vehicle would take at least ten minutes to warm above freezing. She always thought about the luxury of a remote starter after a long day. She would add this to her wish list. The roads were salted, and the traffic was thick but moving. She would take it steady as she did not want anything to ruin this time off. She finally turned into her street and then carefully into her driveway. The driveway was partially plowed. Emily managed to maneuver her car around the piled snow and into the garage. She got out of the car, still in her scrubs, and grabbed her bag. She was home.

Luke was not home yet from work as his car was not parked in the garage. This was a novelty as she was usually thinking up apologies on her way home from work, to cover for her habitual lateness. Mrs Lundgren was just getting Oliver and Rachel down from the table. There were crumbs on the floor and spilt milk on the table. Rachel shouted, "Mommy," when she saw her coming into the kitchen. She ran toward Emily with her sticky baby fingers and outstretched arms, reaching up with great enthusiasm. Oliver looked over and smiled but then returned to his Legos. He seemed subdued, sitting amongst a kaleidoscope of toys, focusing on a missing wheel from his Lego car. The house was in its usual controlled chaos. Emily wished she had the time and energy to clean her house more thoroughly, she just didn't. Her family was far more expert at messing it up than she was at cleaning it up. Luke usually managed the laundry, but the rest was generally left for Emily. She would put forth a valiant effort when she had her golden weekend — the one weekend a month where a resident would get two days off in a row — sandwiched between two on-call days. Emily would frantically clean and cook on these days. She would manage the kids' baths and bedtimes stories, savoring the ordinariness of it all. Emily felt she was playing house at these times, pretending this was their lives. A normal stay-at-home mom spending time with her family. She was fully aware that it was not just the resident who paid the price, but also their families. They would also reap the benefits, eventually.

Typically, Mrs Lundgren would tidy up the larger messes. Her given name was Sarah, she had a formal manner which made first names awkward. Emily had waited for her to ask to be addressed by her first name, but this never came. She had spent her life as a homemaker and nanny but easily could have been a CEO of a company, had she been born in a different time, family and place. She was organized, intelligent and efficient in her approach. Mrs Lundgren seemed even more formal recently. Emily knew the change in her demeanor co-occurred with Luke becoming more distant and, as a result, Mrs Lundgren had the kids with growing frequency. Luke had not been himself for a long time. He was often withdrawn and moody. Other times he seemed to be in a daze and irrational. He was spending more time in his office when he was home. Emily had walked in on him writing, what appeared to be a letter, but he suddenly stopped writing and seemed slightly embarrassed. He looked so sad at times, but she just could not reach him. Or maybe she just hadn't tried hard enough. Emily was secretly thankful that Mrs Lundgren was with the children. However, this seemed to be taking its toll on Sarah. Especially with her own predicaments.

Mrs Lundgren's prodigal daughter was visiting from North Carolina. Her daughter was around Emily's age and had seen a fair amount of misfortune. Much of it of her own making from the limited information shared with her by Mrs Lundgren. Her daughter, Abigail, had recently come out of rehab for drug abuse. She had been addicted to a variety of drugs including methamphetamine and opiates. Some illegal and some prescription medications. She was not particularly discriminating with her form of escape. Emily knew she had been either a high school cheerleader captain or prom queen or something similar. From the many photographs that Mrs Lundgren had around her home, Abby was small and blonde with large soulful green eyes. Emily was not given the details of her descent into the pharmacological abyss. She knew that she had been married once, but he left her for a close friend. She had pursued relief for this betrayal in numerous self-destructive ways. These had included a succession of progressively more insalubrious relationships. There was certainly greater pain and reasons for her choices than presented on the surface. As an outsider you can only fill in the gaps of knowledge with a seemingly rational interpretation. It is, of course, grossly flawed and mostly inaccurate, but it serves to satisfy some of the ghoulish curiosity generated by tragedy. It is too tempting to create our own narratives even with those we think we know most completely. Mrs Lundgren assured Emily that Abby was 'clean' and that she would be an asset. Sometimes Emily would agree to pay Mrs Lundgren and her daughter, so Sarah would be able to watch the children. This adding to their weekly costs. Luke had generally been responsible for paying Mrs Lundgren, which was one less task for Emily. Emily was truly thankful for Mrs Lundgren.

Not burdening Sarah further, Emily would call Amy to water her sickly plants while they were away. Amy was a neighbor and one of the few work colleagues that Emily had developed a kind of friendship. Amy was newly single and a fellow resident. Emily would cover her shifts on occasion and knew Amy would help Emily out in a pinch. Emily had not made use of this arrangement previously. Amy had messy shoulder length brown hair, pale skin, a sharp, fine nose and black horn-rimmed glasses which gave the impression of a disheveled professor. The overall effect was endearing. She always looked post-call, even after her golden weekend. She was invaluable and had been a great support. She was one of the few people with whom Emily could be completely honest. This had become important as her discussions with Luke had become increasingly fraught and infrequent.

Hopefully, this week would help to reunite them as a family, as a couple. She kissed Rachel's face and held her tight. It felt so good to hold her babies. It was like an itch which needed to be scratched. Oliver had already made his way back into the living room where further toys were strewn all over the floor. Legos. Oliver was fair like his dad, but with Emily's serious and analytical character. He also inherited her kindness. Rachel was dark like her mom and with her inquisitive mind, but with her dad's outgoing and passionate disposition. Oliver would seem to be pondering things so intensely that Emily would be in awe of his concentration. Emily could not fathom what would engross a preschooler so completely. Emily needed to shower and to pack, but right now she wanted to sit on the floor and play with Oliver and Rachel. She did not look forward to the flight with the kids. However, she and Luke could each manage one child on the flight. Emily was enjoying being with the children when she glanced at her phone and noticed the time. Where was Luke? It was after seven. She had cleaned up the floor and the table and was just about ready to run the baths for the kids, with her anxiety increasing with each minute. She was about to call Luke when she thought she could hear his ancient Range Rover pull up in the driveway. He came in looking sheepish. He said he needed to tie up loose ends at work before the trip, avoiding her gaze. This doing little to allay her unease. Emily kissed him on the cheek and headed for the shower. "Good, Luke, you can get Oliver and Rachel into the bath and bed. Rachel wants you to read *Violet's House* and you can ask Oliver what he wants you to read to him." With this, she grabbed her robe and headed for the bathroom.

Chapter 3
Travel and Ruminations

Packing for four people for a week was not for the fainthearted, especially when hunting down summer clothes and having to wash most items. They had Target in Orlando, right. When each person had sufficient clothing to last a couple of days including changes due to spillage and imprecise self-feeding techniques, Emily decided that the packing was done. The carry-on still needed to be organized with enough snacks, toys, diapers, wipes etc.... Tickets and seat and itinerary to be readily available electronically. When all of this was finished Emily would get around four hours of sleep before they needed to be up and out. She did not care — they were going to be together for an entire week. She fell asleep still smiling. Morning arrived far too quickly. Rachel and Oliver were crying over getting ready so early. Both in rebellion when it came to wearing their winter coats and boots. She relented and let them wear their shoes and for Rachel to wear her princess ballet shoes — threadbare. You pick your battles. Emily smiled at Rachel. Matching clothes and appropriate shoes are very much overrated. Everything was so rushed that Emily had not yet spoken to Luke more than about the plan of attack to get their family in one piece to Orlando. Her kids were still too young to enjoy the theme parks, but they got a cheap villa from one of Luke's colleagues. He had a timeshare, but he could not get away from the office this week, fortunately Emily and Luke could. It had a pool and a barbecue. Heaven. Once on the plane and with both kids quietly sleeping, Emily looked over at Luke. His dirty blond hair, which needed cutting, and piercing blue eyes, still caused a flutter in her heart. He had the most beautiful smile Emily had ever seen. It was ever so slightly crooked and started slowly until it lit up his entire face. He had symmetric white teeth with a small gap in between his front teeth which served to add to the charm. He was good looking in a relaxed tousled way, but his smile ramped this up to being drop dead gorgeous. He would often use this weapon when he knew that he had lost an argument or to soften his opponent. Usually, Emily these days. She would often make fun of his age, only two years her senior, but he was older, nonetheless. He was looking even older over the past months with dark circles under his eyes. He also seemed to have lost weight as his jeans were far looser than she remembered. She had not really seen him in a very long time. His shirt holding onto the remnants of cheerios and juice. Most likely grape from the appearance of the stain. She loved this man. They had met at college. He had a kind of easiness to him that attracted Emily. She had come from a disconnected family with an alcoholic and abusive stepfather and then a single parent family. She had been wary of people to avoid being hurt. Opening her wounds for others to see. She had deliberately avoided close relationships. This had made her both vulnerable and invulnerable simultaneously.

Luke had made her laugh. His easy manner and outgoing style made their relationship natural and seamless. He had been in her political science class and seemed to ask those questions that no one had thought of, but once they were out, no one could understand how they could proceed without knowing the answer. He would smile at Emily and eventually asked her out for coffee. He seemed so nonchalant about it all. Later he would tell Emily that he had practiced in front of a mirror for hours before he finally approached her. They had an easy rapport. It was the rare combination of effortlessness and longing. He had been attracted to Emily's single-mindedness and sense of humor. Her reticence making her slightly mysterious. The mystery for Emily was trying to hide her past and brokenness. Their relationship was smooth and warm. When they finally fully committed to one another it felt right and healing. How did he know to tread so carefully? To show so much grace. This was the first time Emily did not have to resist youthful fumblings, and simply be herself. Raw and exposed. At times, she felt so exposed she would have to fight the urge to look away and retreat. But his innocent, open confidence in their love prevented her from doing so. She felt connected to Luke and he was to her. He encouraged her through the rigors of medical school and then her residency, having two children in the midst of all the pandemonium. He believed in her, even when she was so uncertain in herself. She could endure the heavy responsibility, the sleep deprivation, and the catastrophic financial burden, if they could hold together. She did not need many people, but those she let in were forever burned into her heart.

She would also hold Luke together during their journey. When his mother was sick and even more when she died after a long and heartbreaking course of disease. When he was disappointed with his career progress, and when he wanted to carve out a larger slice of 'me time' to re-establish his identity. They had carried each other through the 'realness' of life. Luke also held back, she suspected, and later, fully discovered. Emily did not push him as she knew that we all have pages in our own stories that we tear out and others we encrypt, 'lest any know us quite'. Just because you love someone does not mean there are no vulnerabilities too great to be completely laid bare. It is an evolutionary process. They both allowed each other this space. Emily knew that his father had left when he was in elementary school. His mom had raised him alone. He had an older brother, but they didn't have any contact. His older brother left when Luke was in middle school. Luke was bright, but not overly motivated. She loved his casual seriousness about life. He was tall and lean. He liked poetry, the classics rather than modern poetry. He was from Chicago and had a lot of acquaintances but few close friends. Maybe this was part of the adhesive that had bound them together in their previous life. The simplicity of their inter-dependence.

Rachel's sleepy smile and murmurings interrupted her thoughts. She could see the mischief in the semi-awake eyes. She said, "Mommy, drink." Emily got her sippy cup out and poured water into the cup. Rachel grabbed the cup and drank greedily. She put her chubby fingers together to gesture for 'more' although she was quite capable of saying the word. Emily refilled the cup and was fully back in the moment of practicalities. Oliver, who was still sleeping on Luke's lap, also began to stir. The captain was announcing the descent into Orlando and beeps indicating instructions to 'return to your seat' and 'buckle your seatbelt' signs. So far, so good. Florida, here we come.

Chapter 4
Reconnecting and Vacation

They navigated the airport with relative ease. The car was procured and were on their way to the villa. It was warm and green. Emily reached for Luke's hand, but he pulled away ever so slightly before squeezing her hand. They would have time to reconnect later, she thought hopefully. They pulled into the small driveway. It was your typical stucco semi-detached villa. Pink, so Rachel was happy. They carried their luggage into the bedrooms. There was a pool and Emily was already checking out the sturdiness of the locks on the patio doors. Everything else was in nondescript shades of beige. The patterned tan carpet would hopefully hide the inevitable stains made by her children. She saw a welcome pack with cookies, juice boxes, bottled water, crayons, and cleaning products. An unusual mix. In the refrigerator, there was a half-gallon of unopened milk which was still in date. Emily cleaned Rachel's sippy cup and grabbed a cup for Oliver. She would give them some cookies and milk and put them both down for a nap. They were both cooperative with the plan as they had not achieved their usual ten hours of sleep even with the napping on the flight. Once they were asleep, Emily went into the bedroom to talk to Luke, but he too was asleep. Emily put on her bathing suit and went for a swim to clear her head. The cool water felt good. The gentle slapping down of her arms and then dividing the water. She was lost in the calming rhythmic motion of her body against the slick liquid. She was thinking about Luke and how distant he seemed. She was not sure how long this was the case as she hadn't been paying close attention. Initially, she was almost happy when he stopped asking what time she was going to be home. Now it just felt lonely. How do you undo neglect? Emily had not meant to take Luke for granted, but it had all been so much to manage. Overwhelming at times. She would comfort herself with the fact that her residency would eventually end, and they would be a normal family. She would not have lives urgently depending on her. She would still have great responsibility, but not all the time. She could refer to specialists or to the ED in emergencies or to her juniors. She could share the load. Not feel her back was breaking under the weight. Home was where all things would lead. Her dreams revolved around her family and their intertwined futures. So why do medicine? This was the culmination of years of study and work. She genuinely wanted to make a difference. To be with people during those vulnerable times. To make someone better, to heal. Her experiences had made her uniquely qualified. She enjoyed the mental challenges as well. Emily had lived through so many tragedies that she would not look away no matter how painful. She would not disengage because she did not know how to answer the pain in someone's eyes. The confusion with the loss of someone just snatched away without warning. Emily would let them talk and talk until they were finished. She would listen to the cries and screams. The murmurings. She would absorb the pain. She also loved the victories when lives were saved. When someone leaving the hospital was more miracle than skill. How could she explain the complex and conflicting experiences to her family? Why she did not want to have long conversations about the day-to-day rhetoric. The mundane happenings in our lives. The fillers while we are planning our futures. Emily would try and sometimes even be engaged in the small talk. However, her mind would inevitably be drawn back to the lives at the hospital. Each failure etched into her memory; the victories faded. To try and understand why a life needed to end and whether some feat could have reversed this conclusion. The tears when this occurred, sometimes the weariness making them impossible to shed. They just remained as a cold lump in her chest. Another journey cut short. She would ask God, but their relationship had been strained for many years. She had not expected a response., But sometimes she just did not know where else to go. Or who else to blame.

Luke called to Emily asking if she was all right. "Hi, I didn't hear you get up."

"Do you want a drink?" Luke asked.

"Sure, what's on offer?"

Luke smiled and answered, "Water, milk or juice box." Emily made her way out of the water and threw a towel over her shoulders after a haphazard attempt at drying her wet body. She sat down casually on one of the loungers.

Emily smiled. "Juice box please." Her demeanor suddenly changing and becoming sober. "Luke, what's going on?" Emily said quietly.

"What's going on where?" said Luke, averting his eyes from Emily. He had forgotten how perceptive she was. He tried to shield himself from her penetrating brown eyes. He knew he could not lie to her, at least not directly. Emily wanted to discuss this further but was interrupted by the cacophony of both children waking at the same time.

"Mommy!"

"Mommy!" Emily finished drying herself off and went into the villa.

They had developed a pattern in how they spent their days. Waking up and having breakfast, going out to a park or shops or the beach. They would have a snack out and return in the late afternoon for a swim and then dinner. They would vary this with an occasional restaurant or having a barbecue and eating at the villa. Both children were usually asleep before their book of choice had been read. Luke had evaded all but the most benign questions. Their ease with one another was slowly returning despite this fact.

Emily was drifting off to sleep and woke to Luke's loud laughter coming from the living room. It had been a long time since she heard him laugh with such pleasure. She smiled from the infectious nature of his joyfulness. He was laughing at a mildly funny commercial, but he could not stop. Emily started laughing and they were both uncontrollable for several minutes. It was like a valve had been opened with the release of blissful hilarity. When they had gained control, he pulled her close and kissed her deeply. She felt her long-forgotten feelings for him reawaken. She had closed her eyes and lifted her face for another kiss, but he stopped abruptly and pulled away. Emily was left feeling hurt and confused. Luke had reverted to the distant man she had come to expect. The transformation had been so gradual that she hardly noticed it at first. Initially he had just stopped doing the trivial things like watching her favorite shows with her. Not wanting to go with her separate from the children, not caring when she came home. Then he would take ever so slightly longer before coming to bed. He would be in the same room, but the isolation was profound. He stopped missing her. Emily tried not to care. When she pushed it, he pulled out the guilt card. He had to take care of the children and the domestic responsibilities. Although Emily still carried more than her fair share of the burden, she would yield, reminded once again of her own imperfections. It always felt she was failing someone. It had become the backdrop of her life. Despite these truths, Emily was determined to force the issue on this trip as he had escalated his reclusive and irritable behaviors. She was genuinely concerned about him. About their family.

Emily's thoughts were suspended by the phone ringing. She was not going to answer as she was quite sure no one was calling for them. She ignored it as long as she could, but the call was not going to voice mail. She answered the phone and was met with silence and then a dial tone. This happened for three consecutive calls. Emily would answer and say, "Hello", and then there was silence and again they would hang up.

The fourth occasion Emily was expecting the same process but instead was met with a deep quiet voice. "Hi is Luke Wilson there? Tell him it's Tony. Tony Dupont."

"No, I'm sorry but there isn't a Luke Wilson here." Emily said.

"Oh, sorry to have disturbed you, ma'am," he said before he hung up.

Emily turned to Luke who now appeared skittish. "Luke, do you know anyone here? A Tony Dupont? Were you expected to work while we are here?"

"No, should I?" Luke responded defensively.

"Someone just called several times. They hung up the first three times and then he asked for a Luke Wilson," Emily said.

Luke was visibly pale. "I am sure it was a wrong number, there is more than one 'Luke W' in the world. If it had been work, they would have got my name right, don't you think?"

"Don't you think it is too much of a coincidence to ask for a 'Luke' at all?" Emily answered feeling the all too familiar conflict returning.

"I must be pretty important if random people are looking for me," Luke said with his crooked smile and most sincere looking gaze. "I am going to get some cereal and bread. I'll be back later," Luke said hastily. He sounded as though he was trying to be calm but looked pale and sweaty.

"Luke, we are not done talking about this." But he was already opening the door to leave. He waved his hand above his head as he left.

He avoided her gaze when he returned. Emily assumed he wanted the time away to have a break from domestic life but was more than a little hurt by his evasion. She felt as though she had been overly suspicious. He was right, why would random people be calling an accountant? Emily pushed it from her mind but the uneasiness in the pit of her stomach remained.

The week ended far too quickly. Emily and Luke had just started to re-couple. They were sharing experiences rather than just work. Once you had been through so much life together there seems to be a natural synchronizing of affections if the time is allowed. A sort of modified non-locality principle, they could remain in sync no matter how far their distance. They did love each other and their children, whatever else may be. During the flight home, Emily caught Luke looking at her, when she gazed back at him, his eyes held the tenderness that had been lost and he said quietly, "I love you, Emily. You are way too good for me, you always have been." He reached for her hand and kissed it softly. "I am going to make things right."

"What things?" Emily asked quietly, uncertain of what 'things' he was referring to. There were so many. Before he could answer, the captain announced their descent into Minneapolis-St Paul International airport.

Soon the controlled mayhem and guilt would return. She watched the blanket of grey-white snow loom larger as they approached the MSP airport. She felt a transient dread come over her as they descended onto the landing strip.

Chapter 5
Luke

*O*nce back at work, their usual routines returned. Emily spent long hours in the clinic. She was thankful to have this month of outpatient as there could be more of a rhythm to life rather than the frenzied chaos of the hospital. It was only a week ago but seemed somewhere in the distant past. She could not reconnect with Luke. She tried to re-establish dialogue, but he would inevitably divert or deflect the conversation. She could tell that sometimes he also wanted to communicate, but he resisted opening up. More reclusiveness in his office, writing and more writing. She had more time to think about it and it was making her increasingly frustrated. This is not how they solved their problems. They had come too far on this journey to stop talking now. Emily tried to come home as close to her expected time as was feasible. She would ask him about his day and tried to engage in any area of common ground. This was getting too hard. Sometimes Emily's loneliness was palpable and all encompassing. Like Luke, she did not have close family or a lot of close friends. Luke was her best friend and her family. How could he be so reckless with this fact? Emily was fully aware of the struggles taking care of their children and their lives. How he must have felt abandoned and isolated. This is marriage, sometimes the journey is effortless and other times you barely make it through. Not knowing how you did it, when looking back.

It was the home stretch, but Luke had wondered whether it would ever really be the 'home stretch'. He had become weary with this promise. He loved Emily and her passion for those in her world. She was beautiful, in a no make-up, fresh faced kind of way. Luke just was not sure whether he fitted into her world any longer. Or whether he even wanted to. He did not want to hurt Emily or disrupt the kids' lives, but he was finished with feeling like 'the help', rather than a partner. The doctor's spouse. The failed bard. Luke had never really wanted children; they just sort of happened. This had been the story of his life, things just happening rather than deliberate planning. He had been forced to take care of his mother. He loved her, but she had always taken care of him. He really felt ill-equipped to return the generosity. Initially, he would go over to her house and talk to her. He would tell her about his day and sometimes bring the kids over, mostly Oliver as Rachel was still a baby. He then needed to take her to her appointments and grocery shopping. It evolved into him having to pick up her medications and to make her food to eat. He would clean her up when she had become too frail to make it to the bathroom. She had a nurse come in three times a week and home care, but not nearly enough. She did not want to leave her home, but did suggest this towards the end, to give Luke an out. She would cry out in pain if she thought Luke would not hear her. He felt so out of his depth, he did not know how he could even begin to ask for help. Who would he ask? Luke had to deal with his mother's deteriorating health on his own. He was failing again. He did contact his older brother, but they had never been close, and he did not respond to his letter in any case. Luke told his mother that he could not find the address, when she asked about her favored son. Luke was there to carry out menial tasks and to give her pain medication, to be useful. And also, to avoid looking into her eyes and seeing the magnitude of her anguish. He would have been voted in high school as being the least likely person to take care of any living thing. Life was full of irony. His mother eventually died last year. The cancer consuming her body until only an emaciated shell remained. Her last days were spent either delirious or in pain, and sometimes both. He would never get those images out of his head. He could never let himself feel so much pain again. And so impotent.

His mother had been optimistic for him when he was a teenager, and he could feel the weight of her disappointment with how he had lived his life. He could never quite measure up to her exacting standards. That was all before she was ill. It all changed. She had far simpler ambitions for her son and for herself as her illness progressed. She wanted to fight the cancer and then she wanted to live past certain dates, relevant only to her. Eventually, she would only want to escape the pain, no matter how brief. To say, "I love you", without grimacing so some remnant of her former self would be recollected when she was gone.

His time was divided between taking care of the children and his mother. He added part-time accounting work to the exhausting mix. His choices were again restricted and not of his volition. Recently, he had been taking more time for himself. It felt good. He found he could escape sometimes without leaving his mother. This continued into everyday life. One little pill.

He was enjoying his time away from Emily and the kids more than he cared to admit. Not to be reminded of his failings. To be compared to other men and found wanting. His secrets were mounting. He kind of liked having a dichotomous existence. It made him feel important. Although, he had increasingly wanted greater autonomy, he was no longer satisfied with slivers of time for himself. He wanted chunks of time or even large wedges of decadent, self-indulgent time. He wanted freedom to make his own choices. To travel 'The road not taken'. He loved that poem.

> *Two roads diverged in a yellow wood,*
> *And sorry I could not travel both,*
> *And be one traveler, long I stood,*
> *And looked down one as far as I could,*
> *To where it bent in the undergrowth...*
> *I shall be telling this with a sigh*
> *Somewhere ages and ages hence:*
> *Two roads diverged in a wood, and I,*
> *I took the one less traveled by,*
> *And that has made all the difference.*
> - Robert Frost.

Luke regretfully looked down the road he had not taken. What could have been if he had not the responsibilities for other lives. He missed reading for the sheer pleasure of the words and phrases woven into intricate tapestries with rich colors and subtle hues. Each phoneme offering delicious promise. The fabric could be worked and reworked to create a new evolving vestment. The lovely wistful sonnets. He had given this up because he was fairly good at numbers and he had a greater chance of making money with accounting. Boring, tedious, accounting. No declarations of undying love or paths not traveled, but only numbers, representing the very concrete world where we lived out our daily lives. He deserved to be happy. He only wished he had the clarity of mind and courage to achieve his aspirations. One more pill to numb the pain.

Emily had helped with his mother, but only for brief fragments of time. She did not understand the burden he faced or, if she did, she had not conveyed this information to Luke. There were times when they did not say anything, but they would hold each other until dawn. Luke could not tell Emily about his demons that tormented his mind and she allowed him the space of this comfortless and distraught chamber. She never pressed him. He was unsure whether this was due to discretion or her lack of strength to open the door. These occasions seemed a lifetime ago. Now they both turned away from one another, the distance between them an insurmountable gulf. Emily pretended to be asleep when he left with his suitcase for Atlanta for an accountants' conference. Last night at dinner, he said he was looking forward to meeting some key players in his company. He was more tender with her when he said goodbye; regarding her more thoughtfully. Emily felt the intensity but was distracted by the mayhem of the morning. She was encouraged by Luke's sudden willingness to take an interest in his default career. And in 'learning about the newest business software' which would make his life so 'much easier'. Overall, he had settled into a mercurial existence. Luke had become more confident, almost too confident and then he would withdraw into himself. It was hard to keep up with who he was going to be from day to day. One more pill. One more hit.

Chapter 6
Journey Cut Short

This morning was like any other morning. The snow was slowly melting, and the grey skies were giving way to pale blue. It no longer hurt to go outside from the piercing cold. Almost spring. Rachel and Oliver, still sleepy and cranky, were getting dressed and then consuming their breakfasts. Rachel spilling the milk from her bowl but eating the cheerios. Emily was waiting for Mrs Lundgren to appear. Emily had clinic but her first patient was not scheduled until nine a.m. She had the luxury of time this morning. It was still hectic but in a controlled fashion. She was only pulled in one direction. Mrs Lundgren arrived, and Emily left with only a few cries of protest. Mrs Lundgren said she needed to discuss their arrangement when Emily came home from work. Emily agreed, but did not have time to go into this further. Emily kissed the children and left for clinic. Despite the problems she and Luke were having, the warmer weather lightened her mood. The journey to the clinic was uneventful and Emily was able to nab one of the coveted parking spaces in front of the clinic, a tired-looking 1970s tan brick edifice. Maybe everything would be okay. Her schedule was full, mostly follow up patients she would see apart from Dr

Meyer. He was the attending physician, a kindly older gentleman who still wore a bow tie. He could appear to be clumsy at times but was a brilliant physician. Emily had never allowed herself the arrogance of some of her contemporaries had when working with him. It was a foolish mistake to make, to confuse social awkwardness with a cognitive deficit, and he would make note of such behaviors. He had a long memory, especially when selecting those being put forward for attending positions. Some of the other residents had come from backgrounds of privilege and found humility a difficult skill to learn. Virtually all would learn this skill at some point in their career. Sometimes easier and sometimes harder, but it would be learned. Emily understood humility from the onset. This helped later, but was a hindrance initially, when all were actively competing with one another. Emily never did get the hang of emphasizing her achievements. It felt cringey and childish. There is a clear order to medicine. The senior runs the team most of the time with the intern being used strategically in case the senior cannot get to more than one serious situation at a time. The medical students are guided through the history and physical examinations and the paperwork. They pay extraordinary amounts of money for this privilege. The attendings are in command, the ultimate aspiration of the resident and medical student. The Holy Grail, so to speak. Pondering this hierarchy, Emily was surprised to find her patient charting was completed. And before lunchtime no less. The time had flown by. She had forgotten to bring a lunch today, so she would forage from the staff room snacks. She shoved a five-dollar bill into the snack fund, and retrieved two bite-sized Snickers bars, Goldfish crackers, and a diet Dr Pepper. So much for a nutritious diet. She would eat a healthy dinner later. The rest of the afternoon was uneventful. Emily was hopeful to leave around six p.m., once patients were all seen, the results were reviewed, phone calls were made, and encounters charted. She left the clinic while there was still fading daylight. This was encouraging. She would stop by the grocery store on the way home and pick up a pie for dessert. She planned on making stir-fry with vegetables and chicken and cherry pie for dessert. Low sugar cherry pie, she promised herself to try to stick to the 'healthier' dinner. Anything was better than hospital food. Emily had not thought much about food today but was suddenly famished and salivating over the taste of the prospective dinner. On her drive home Emily usually had the radio on, mostly as mindless noise, but also to keep up with any relevant local news. She had mentally shut down and driving on autopilot when she had heard about a car crash off A14 in Anoka. She felt a chill down the back of her neck when the announcer was describing the incident. She was left to wonder whether there were any children involved, a mother, a grandfather... Emily liked to understand the story behind the tragedies. She had seen countless of these life changing events with her many emergency room rotations. It becomes almost routine. To combat a developing callousness, Emily tried to know the story behind each tragedy. If you knew the story it made the event more human. More dignified and real. This made the pain sharper, but it was worth the exchange. Indifference for humanity. However, towards the end of her last rotation, the fatigue, and the vast number of traumas, had caused some callouses to form. This was survival.

Emily was turning onto her road looking forward to seeing the kids. She was missing Luke already. Getting away for the week reminded her that they were a couple as well as being a family. She would make the time to talk to Luke when he got back, maybe book a hotel away for the weekend. Amy could watch Oliver and Rachel and they could work on the couple part, without the interruptions of daily life. Emily was abruptly brought into the present with the assault of flashing blue lights in front of her house. At first, she thought it was the neighbor's house but then she could see the sheriff's car parked in the driveway. She felt her heart race as she hastily abandoned her car in front of the house. All she could think of was that something had happened to Oliver or Rachel. She felt relief when she saw them both fighting with each other. Mrs Lundgren was trying to comfort and quiet their desperate cries. Emily ran to Oliver and Rachel and gathered them up into her arms.

"Mommy, Oliber won't gib me the car," Rachel bellowed.

Emily said, "You both need to share," and handed a car to each of them, which seemed to work as they were somewhat quieted. Emily then looked to see the sheriff standing in the living room. His face grim.

"Hello, ma'am. I am Sheriff Davis with the Anoka County Sheriff's department." He cleared his throat and inquired as to who she was.

"I am Emily Warrington. What's going on?" said Emily with rising panic.

"Do you know a Mr Lucas Warrington?" Sheriff Davis asked deliberately.

"He's my husband." Emily could feel her stomach contract and the nausea rising into her throat.

"I think it would be best if you sat down, ma'am," he offered. Obediently, Emily sat down. Pulling Oliver and Rachel onto her lap, with both children struggling for the most room. Emily called Mrs Lundgren over to take the children into Oliver's room. Rachel was pleased as usually Oliver would not let her in his room after she had destroyed his favorite cars.

"Mrs Warrington, I am afraid your husband has been in a serious accident." Sheriff Davis said this slowly to allow the information to penetrate. He hated this part of the job, but he had become relatively adept at presenting the macabre material. "Mr Warrington's car was hit by a semi-truck on the A14 near Anoka."

"What," was all Emily could muster. Her mind was racing, and she felt like she could not breathe.

"Mr Warrington has been in a serious accident. Is there anyone I can call to help?"

Emily shook her head not quite processing what he was trying to say. "Is he, all right?" Although Emily already knew the answer, she could not let herself contemplate that unthinkable possibility.

"I am afraid Mr Warrington had severe injuries. His injuries were, in fact, catastrophic. I am afraid he didn't survive the accident. They did all that they could to save him at the scene and at the county hospital." He was speaking and looking over her shoulder to avoid looking directly into her eyes. "It appeared that he went instantly so he didn't suffer. I am so sorry for your loss." And he truly was.

"No! No!" Emily screamed. It couldn't be Luke. "He is in Atlanta; it must be someone else."

"Mrs Warrington, I need you to come with me to the hospital to identify the bod..." He hesitated before saying, "Mr Warrington."

Mrs Lundgren was standing in the doorway. "I'll stay with the children," she offered. Emily felt too shaky to drive, she didn't want to ride with the sheriff. The only person she could think of was Amy.

Time was almost standing still. Everything was surreal and seemingly in slow motion. Emily reached for her cell phone and dialed Amy. "Amy, this is Emily, they're saying that Luke has been in an accident. I need to identify him." Emily could hardly get those words out. They didn't seem to be words, but just sounds, until they were said. Emily was surprised as those words came out, as if she were telling herself as well as Amy.

"What do you need me to do?" Amy asked, still not clear on what Emily was saying.

"Could you take me to the hospital?"

"Of course, I will be over in five," said Amy.

Amy appeared looking more scruffy than usual but, true to her word, in five minutes. She drove an old, dilapidated jeep. Emily felt as though she was in a daze; it couldn't be Luke. He was in Atlanta. It must be some mistake. Amy kept quiet for most of the journey, leaving Emily to battle her thoughts. Amy knew where to go once they arrived at the county hospital. She had completed many rotations in the emergency department or 'ED' during her residency. She went to the ED and asked where Luke Warrington was being held. The nurse asked who she was in relation to Mr Warrington. This question jolted Emily fully alert to answer that she was his wife. The nurse looked away and said she would be right back with the attending. Emily saw the chairs in the waiting room but could not sit down, she wanted to run away. The attending, looking pale and tired, came through the doors. He asked which one was Mrs Warrington. Emily said that she was his wife. He asked them both to come into the family room. Emily knew what this meant. She walked slowly as if delaying the conversation and the knowledge could help her brain absorb what was going to be said.

"Mrs Warrington, your husband has been in a devastating accident and we couldn't save him despite out best efforts. His injuries were just too great and he had lost too much blood." Dr Edwards continued quietly. "I am very sorry, ma'am."

"Where is he?" Emily uttered almost to herself.

"He is in the stabilization room," he answered plainly. "We kept him there until you were able to see him. To identify him. Would you like to go back now?" Emily just nodded. They walked through the ED as she had many times in the past. She recognized some of the doctors and the nurses, all busy with patients, charts, vitals etc. The noises and bustle of a county hospital emergency department. The movements and sounds seemed to be a part of some low budget movie. All with predictable characters and obvious plotlines. Going about their business of how the scenes were going to be played out for the casualties and their families.

The stabilization room, or 'stab room', still had the gruesome reminders of the war that had just taken place. The lost battle for life. The room in disarray reflecting the violence of defeat. Units of blood given, needles and empty vials of epinephrine on the tray and on the floor. Emily saw a covered figure on the table. Dr Edwards pulled back the sheet that had obscured his face. Emily gasped and then drew her hands to her mouth. Luke's face was bruised and swollen but this was definitely Luke. His sandy hair with streaks of black due to dried blood. A purple induration and laceration over his left eye. Emily went over to touch his face, it was no longer warm, it no longer held any expression. It already looked more like wax than flesh. She would never kiss his lips again or brush his hair out of his eyes. Her head was spinning, how could this be? Last night he had slept beside her. He held Oliver on his lap. They would work things out. No! This could not be Luke. Emily thought she was going to faint. She could not breathe. She stumbled but Amy prevented her from falling. Amy, who had told families about the death of their loved ones, could not begin to comprehend the loss of Luke for Emily. Emily reached for his hand; she couldn't see his wedding ring. Emily demanded to know where his wedding ring was. Dr Edwards said it was with his personal effects.

Dr Edwards left and reappeared with a nurse holding a clear plastic bag with car keys, a wallet, and a white gold wedding ring, with 'L&E' inscribed. Emily signed the forms and held the bag limply. The effects were Luke's. Emily felt waves of nausea roll over her again. She could not think. How can you be gone Luke? How can you be gone! Tears started to flow from Emily's eyes. She seemed unaware of their presence as the rivulets made their way down her cheeks. She reached out for Luke's hand again. She wanted to remain connected to him for as long as possible. The cold lifeless hand. She felt her throat constrict in the panic of the moment. She realized that Oliver and Rachel were now fatherless. How could she tell them and cause them so much pain? Emily stood there staring into nothingness with the imprints of her tears leaving their tracks over her face. Amy reached out to touch Emily's shoulder. Emily would need to start the process of disengagement. She would leave the man she loved, the father of her children, her friend, and go to her children. She was still in a state of disbelief. When she finally let his hand drop to his side, the pain was only beginning. Trickling at first but would swell into a full tsunami of torment once the complete force of his loss was grasped.

Emily walked next to Amy, but not acknowledging her presence. Emily's brain felt numb. They drove in silence. Emily watched the turns down the streets in the darkness. Thinking about earlier that day, her life was not perfect but there was hope. Even in their dysfunctional relationship, there was comfort in the familiarity. Another person who knew your quirks, and who was there for the most simple and profound times of your life. Who thought you looked 'cute' when you were pregnant and could no longer wear normal shoes, but only a variation of slippers due to your swollen feet. Who would go out for late night Chinese food runs. No mystery regarding the swollen feet. Who talked about the future of your children and the banal details of everyday life. One who understood the princess shoes and their importance in getting Rachel out the door in the morning quickly or she would dawdle. You are parts of the same whole. The pain is like that of a phantom limb. You continue to feel the pain of the life and connection that will never be again. These thoughts were too exhausting. Right now, all Emily could think of was how she would tell Oliver and Rachel. Who would she need to call at work to stay home with her children? Emily was still deep in thought when Amy pulled up to the house. Amy asked if she wanted her to go in with her into the house. Emily declined and expressed gratitude for taking her to the hospital. It is amazing how your brain can remember basic manners when it cannot comprehend the magnitude of pain and loss. We revert to our automated response repertoire. The outside lights were left on which cast a yellow glow onto the concrete steps leading to the front door. The door creaked as she opened it, Emily had asked Luke to call someone to fix this, now she remembered this as being one of the last conversations she had had with Luke. About something so ordinary. Emily had seen this played out so many times with patients and their families. You think last conversions or words should be philosophical. Frequently, these words are related to the routine and the practical. Asking for water, for more pain meds, or whether they know where the household or insurance documents are. The ordinary. Most of our lives are spent this way, the perfunctory details that lead one day into the next. You never know when you should say something wise or deep, even with patients who know they have limited time. We live our lives in this very physical world. We only allow ourselves to veer off for brief moments into the more existential for fear we will fall off the tracks connecting our lives to some objective path.

She saw Mrs Lundgren sleeping on the couch. Emily was in two minds whether she should wake her or let her sleep. She had been invaluable as a carer and pseudo-grandmother for the children. Luke's mother was dead, and Emily had not communicated with her own mother for years. The last she heard, she lived in the South. Emily was brought back to the present and the burgeoning black hole in her chest. Emily wished she knew how to get through this anguish. She wished she had a supportive family to help with this pain. She had her children. Her mother could not be included as she had allowed the strings holding them together be worn and tattered. No longer reparable. She missed her so much right now.

Chapter 7
New and Old Wounds

Emily's mother, Beatrice, had sent Christmas cards and an occasional letter, but the distance between them had had seemed wide and fixed. The reckless choices and neediness of her mother had made a relationship with her vexing at best. Their past was filled with the tumultuous complexities of her mother's latest man and abandonment in some form. This had proved both painful and disappointing. Her mother would demonstrate renewed interest in Emily's life and would say that it was the two of them 'against the world' and they would enjoy a routine of Emily meeting her mother at work and walking the mile from her clerical job to home. Home was typically a two-bedroom lower unit of a duplex. Usually stucco. The location changed but the living units looked pretty much the same. Emily remembered Lakeland most clearly. They had moved within the area of that small town for around four years. It was a sleepy town with a lake and seasonal influx of tourists. Her mother did not like apartments as they seemed so 'impersonal'. They could not afford a whole house, hence the duplex as a solution. They would cook together, sometimes Emily would do the cooking as her mother was not an aficionado of food preparation and was usually tired after working all day in any case. Emily would enjoy this ritual as it was one of the happiest times they shared together. Emily thought if she could make the house nice enough and if she could cook well enough, her mother would not need to bring home another abusive man into their lives. These times would usually last around two to three weeks, but on one occasion this lasted for over two months. Absolute bliss. Her mother was beautiful, smart and witty. She loved poetry, like Luke. Beatrice had the exuberance of a child. She had been abandoned by her one true love as a teenager, both literally and metaphorically. The boy and her romanticism. She spent the rest of her life trying to fill this void. Emily's stepfather had been in and out of rehab and jail. Her mother and stepfather had met while her mother was running from the South and working in a dive restaurant as a cook. Irony. Her stepfather had brought them back to Minnesota, where he had family. Beatrice had some cousins in Minnesota, but more of her family were Southern, Emily could not quite remember which area of the South, she seemed to recall some place on the coast, maybe one of the Carolinas. The South had seemed liked one entity with stately homes, warm weather and slow, syrupy accents. Emily had a few happy memories of her stepfather. One memory was when they were on the porch swing. It was a balmy summer evening and she sat between her stepdad and her mother as the swing softly moved back and forth, with the gentle creaking of the worn structure. Her mother had made popcorn, which had way too much butter, but Emily ate it enthusiastically. Her stepdad, Hank, had pointed out the constellations in the summer sky. She remembered this time as she felt safe and valued, nestled between her caregivers. Hank would sometimes bring home treats, frequently out of shame. But most of their interactions had been mixtures of frustration, anger and fear. His drinking had become the center of his world. Emily had nightmares about some of her earliest memories related to Hank and his violence. The fear of listening to the sound of his uneven, sloppy gait and pounding on the front door to get into the house. Emily could feel herself tensing up, knowing it would most likely result in him hitting her mother or herself. He would then pass out on the couch and would be repentant in the morning. Even these memories had faded with the separation of years. Her stepdad also had a tragic upbringing with a mother with mental illness and a mostly absent father. He filled in the blanks on how to be a parent and husband. The scenarios were mostly woven with fragments of movie characters and shadowy distant relatives. The overall effect was choppy and shallow care punctuated with abuse. There were, however, precious moments when their interactions felt real and unique. Emily longed for these encounters and they would sustain her for many months, bathing in the warmth of something that was almost love. Eventually, her mother would tire of Hank and his predictable unpredictability.

    Emily had come to dread the new relationships as they would take precedence over their meager home and resources. Her mother would attend to their every need.

No matter how dysfunctional. She would buy alcohol, make their favorite meals, buy them clothing, get their hair cut. Their rations would be used on someone who barely regarded his generous benefactor. This was until he became bored or she found someone new. They were sometimes violent and almost always verbally abusive. After the last 'boyfriend' stole Emily's babysitting money then threatened to punch her when she demanded he give it back to her, she disengaged. This money that she had saved for over a year. She would count this money and think this could help pay for college. Her mother told her, not to make 'trouble'. Not to make problems for these men. They had sometimes tried to grope her or embarrassed her in front of her friends with crude language. With each abuse she would remain hopeful that they would go and the next time it would be better. If she could be better. This was until her money was stolen, why this and not the cruelties before? There had been far greater injustices, but she had hoped that they were fleeting, and their lives would revert to the joy of just the two of them. Emily just gave up after this last insult. She stopped making dinner. She focused on her grades to create a separate life. A life she could control. Emily had consciously detached from her mother after this last affront. She had learned to be proficient in self-sufficiency.

Emily had been thankful for Mrs Lundgren with her quiet and even disposition. She had offered to watch Oliver when he was a baby and their babysitter had cancelled at the last moment. She had been a stay-at-home mother before her daughter grew up and moved away. She missed the innocence and need of young children.

Mrs Lundgren stirred when Emily went into the kitchen and turned the kettle on. Emily felt drained but could not bring herself to go into her bedroom. Their bedroom. "Are you all right?" asked Mrs Lundgren.

"I don't know," said Emily carefully.

"Did you see Luke?" Mrs Lundgren asked tentatively.

"Yes," Emily answered flatly. "Yes," she said again. "I don't know what I am going to do," Emily said almost to herself.

"Yes, yes, this is a trying time," said Mrs Lundgren. "Let me know how I can help," she said as she patted Emily on the shoulder. This was the closest Sarah had ever come to being affectionate. Emily remembered that Mrs Lundgren had wanted to talk to her. Emily asked what she needed to discuss but Mrs Lundgren had already made her way into the dark and down the path to her car.

Chapter 8
Post-Luke

Emily sat in the dark listening to the whistle of the kettle for what seemed like an eternity, but what was maybe five minutes. The gravity of today's events was coming back in waves. Emily left a message for Dr Meyer's secretary and the residency coordinator that she would not be in for the rest of the week. She was thankful that this was not a call month. She felt panic when she realized the intricate planning she would need to employ to complete her residency. She only had eight weeks left of the residency, she was going to take the attending position at Metropolitan Hospital. How could she ever carry out the responsibilities without Luke? What was he doing here? Why wasn't he in Atlanta? Emily suddenly felt tired and heavy under the weight of these questions and her commission. She threw a pillow and blanket on the couch and fell into a restless sleep. She awoke to Rachel and Oliver jumping on her.

"Mommy you forgot to wake up," Oliver shouted.

Rachel smiled and said, "Maybe Mommy is home!" She then whispered to Oliver, "Don't' tell her 'bout worked."

"Is Daddy home too?" squealed Oliver.

The full force of yesterday's events hit her again. It had taken a few minutes to refresh her memory of the shock of Luke not being there any more. His cold lifeless body. It still seemed a nightmare, not reality. How could Luke, a young and energetic man, be gone? The father of her children? All their plans, their hopes, their dreams. The day-to-day drudgery. It had belonged to them as a family, as a couple. Emily went into the bathroom and wretched.

Oliver said to Rachel, "Mommy is sick that's why she's home."

Emily looked over at Oliver and Rachel with their concerned faces. "I'm okay, you two." Emily could not bring herself to tell them that their father wasn't okay. That he would never be okay. She felt her chest constrict and the tears start to well up. How could he be gone? Emily went into the kitchen and put a K cup into the coffee maker. She listened for the familiar sound of the gurgling and sputtering of the dark liquid dripping into the mug. She put some cereal and milk into a bowl for Oliver and some plain Cheerios in a bowl with a sippy cup full of milk for Rachel. These routine activities were interrupted by her phone. It was Amy. Emily did not want to talk to anyone. She saw the message that she was on her way over. She just wanted to be there with her children and let the unbearable information slowly permeate through her brain, and to her heart. To waver between disbelief and utter anguish. Emily knew that she would have to arrange the funeral and figure out the practicalities that her life without Luke would entail. But not today. Today would be a day of avoidance and stunned silence. She turned on *Paw Patrol* for Oliver and Rachel, so Emily could clear the dishes and clean the table. Emily dropped one of the bowls on the floor and the bowl shattered spilling the residual milk and cereal. Emily felt the hot tears come as she cleaned up the mess on the floor. She sat on the floor unable to summon the strength to get up. How am I going to do this? Her phone again demanded attention with the vibration and Gryllidae ringtone. It was the program director for the residency. This could not be avoided.

"Hello Emily, this is Ashley, I am so sorry to hear about Luke. Amy filled in the details, as I couldn't quite make out what happened from your voice message."

"Thank you," Emily said flatly.

"So, how much time do you think you are going to need?"

"I haven't thought that far ahead, he's only been gone for a day," Emily replied.

"Well, if it is over a couple of weeks you will have to make up the time," Ashley cautioned. "I just wouldn't want you to compromise your attending job." Emily knew that Ashley and several others in her residency were envious of her for getting such a plum job straight out of residency. Emily was certain that Dr Meyer was instrumental in hiring her for the position.

"Thank you, Ashley, for your concern. I will keep you posted." Emily was always fascinated at the shallow and pitiless way Ashley and others like her related to other human beings. Ashley had a special gift for this characteristic. She loved the details. The minutiae of the administrative work which usually caused other residents to groan, would cause Ashley to light up. She loved pointing out the failings in her peers, boosting her self-importance along the way. As long as she could avoid direct patient care, she was happy. She easily detached from the more human aspects of the job. Residents were often treated as work horses, who had the potential to cause other work horses greater burdens. To break the horse's back so to speak. Emily had been shocked by this callousness at first, a resident with a sick child or a dying parent who was ostracized for taking time off. Over time Emily had secretly felt aggrieved at similar scenarios. It would mean being pulled from a desperately needed vacation or non-call month, when you only worked sixty hours a week, or taking away the precious little time from your family. The time that had been so meticulously planned and anticipated. Emily was trying to figure out what she was going to do after this week. It is so unfair that her grief could not be respected and allowed to take its natural course. Those without the luxury of money or time or both. To be allowed to experience the sadness and loneliness that would now become part of her life. At this moment it would seem forever. Their family, although far from perfect, had been somewhat intact. Or at least the illusion of being intact. Emily felt utterly alone. Luke did not have much family, a couple of cousins and uncle from Chicago, a brother living as far away from family as possible. An aunt in Kissimmee. She could find the addresses as she remembered sending thank you cards after Luke's mom, Helen, had died. Emily had kept the list on Luke's computer. The only person who did not respond for Luke's mother's funeral was Luke's older brother.

Emily had gone into their bedroom for fresh clothes as she had slept, or lain down, in the clothes she was wearing. She opened the door and she could see Luke's jacket on the bed, his smell was still in the room. She closed the door and went to find Oliver and Rachel. They were arguing over which *Paw Patrol* character was the best. Rachel liked Skye as she had pink clothes. Rachel was extraordinary in her knowledge of colors, given her young age. Oliver liked Marshall as he put out fires. Emily sat down on the floor and pulled them into her lap. Oliver resisted, and she settled for him sitting next to her. This was her world. These beautiful babies. Still blissfully unaware. Rachel a toddler and Luke would be four next week; she was thankful and saddened by their young ages.

"Mommy why are you sad?" asked Oliver quizzically.

Emily tried to say things in a straightforward way. "Daddy has been hurt and he can't come home any more."

"How was he hurt?" asked Oliver.

"He was in a car accident, and he was hurt very bad."

"Let's see Daddy," said Rachel. "Mommy, fix Daddy," she added.

Oliver asked pensively, "Daddy will still come to my birthday, right? Will we live with Daddy at a different house, like Josh?" Josh was his friend from down the street whose parents divorced last summer.

"No, not like Josh." Emily sighed. "Daddy can't come home any more, he is gone, he's in heaven." Emily choked on the last word.

"Where is heaven?" asked Oliver.

"It is a place above the sky where people go when they die."

"Can we go see Daddy in heaban?" asked Rachel hopefully.

"No, we can't go there," Emily answered simply.

Oliver started crying as his dad had promised him a bike for his birthday. "Now I won't know how to ride a bike, ever," Oliver sobbed. "I want Daddy," cried Oliver louder.

Emily sat there with her children and let the tears fall unchecked, holding them in her arms. "So, do I, Oliver," whispered Emily. Their innocence being so bittersweet. Vacillating between naked self-interests and a profound innocent altruism.

Emily was still on the floor when Amy came into the room. She sat on the floor taking Rachel into her arms and having Rachel wriggle out of them to stand. Rachel put her hands on her hips and said, "Daddy is in heaban and Ollie can't hab a bike. It is bad."

At this, Emily and Amy smiled. "I know, Rach," said Amy with a gentle sigh. Amy asked if they would like to go to the play area at McDonald's as the park was still too muddy with melting snow.

Both kids yelled, "Yes!" as Emily did not often take them to fast food places. Emily was going to protest, but it perished before leaving her lips. She saw how happy it made them and there was so much to do. Emily knew that she could not muster anything like enthusiasm and smiled weakly and hugged each child repeatedly before they pushed her away.

"Bye Mommy," said Rachel. Oliver was already out the door trying to get into Amy's beat-up jeep. He loved her jeep and once even said he would marry her so they could share the vehicle.

Emily went into the office and found the number for Luke's boss to inform him of Luke's death. Death. She still could not say that word without disbelief. She called the main number and asked for Lucas Warrington's direct boss.

"You mean Allen Johnson?"

"Sure," answered Emily.

She was connected to his voice mail. Emily left a message stating that Lucas Warrington was deceased so to send any and all effects to his home address. She would let them know about the funeral arrangements. About an hour later Emily received a call from Allen Johnson. He expressed his condolences and explained that there were no effects at the company as Luke had cleaned out his desk when he was last there. Luke had not been into the office for over two months. Emily asked him to repeat this last statement.

"Luke hasn't been to the office for over two months," repeated Allen. "I am sorry Mrs Warrington."

"What about his trip to Atlanta this week?" said Emily in disbelief.

"Mrs Warrington, Luke had been let go over a month ago. Luke had only completed a fraction of the work he had been contracted to finish. We had allowed him some leeway as he had been a great employee in the past, but since his mother's illness he had produced progressively less work. We tried to be understanding but we had to think about the company. We extended his deadlines at least three times, but he was only able to produce around half of the work, and the product was poorly executed. This was especially the case, over the last couple of months. I truly am sorry, Mrs Warrington, I know Luke was a good man. I wish I could be of more help."

Emily felt nausea rising and the familiar constriction of her throat, making it difficult to breathe. She hastily thanked Allen and ended the call. Her mind was overwhelmed with the loss and now what felt like a further betrayal. Did he feel ashamed that he could not manage his workload? He had always said he wanted more and not less responsibility at work. How could he not tell her? Why did he say he was going to Atlanta? Nothing made sense.

Chapter 9
The Funeral and Other Practicalities

Practicalities of life keep pressing forward whether we are ready or not. Consistent with this, the arrangements for Luke's death proceeded in a blur. Emily had talked with the funeral director and was thankful when he said that they 'would arrange everything', and she should just come in to discuss the preparations. She would need to pay a portion of the cost of the funeral now. Emily had forgotten about the financial aspect of the funeral, again practicalities. He would need four thousand dollars today and the rest when the funeral was organized.

"This of course, won't cover the headstone or the cemetery costs."

Emily said she would come in tomorrow with the check. Lavonne, the funeral director, said that she needed to come in today if she wanted the funeral within the next week. Emily reluctantly agreed. She was waiting for Amy to bring Oliver and Rachel home. She also hoped Amy could come with Emily to the funeral home. She could not face this alone. Her brain was numb. Emily would ask Mrs Lundgren if she could watch the children. She found Mrs Lundgren on her phone and pressed the call button. "Hello, Mrs Lundgren, this is Emily."

Mrs Lundgren hesitated and then responded with a cooler than usual, "What do you need?"

"Could you watch Oliver and Rachel as I need to go to the funeral home for the arrangements? Amy will come with me."

"I guess I could watch them, I know this is a difficult time for all of you," Mrs Lundgren said impassively.

Emily sensed there was more to what Mrs Lundgren was saying than the face value, but she could not think about it now. Her head hurt, and her body hurt, her heart was in shreds. She was hungry but could not choke down anything other than coffee and scraps from the kids. She would try to eat but then the nausea would come. Her head would pound with questions and then the pain. How could he leave us? How could he have left his job? The lies would need to be sifted through, but she felt paralyzed by the gravity and newness of her situation. It was better to ignore her predicament and mechanically go through the process until she could better deal with the disordered details and the pain. Practicalities. Her mind could not do any other. She had to hold it together for Oliver and Rachel or they would not have anyone to hold onto. Emily did not know if she could do this. She felt bruised and empty which was punctuated with deluges of overwhelming grief. This was their lives, day two since Luke's death, D-Two, post-Luke.

Amy arrived just ahead of Mrs Lundgren. Emily looked at Amy and said, "Could you come with me to the funeral home?"

"Sure," Amy replied without hesitation. They drove to the funeral home in silence, each deep in their own thoughts.

They pulled into the driveway of a formal looking funeral home. Emily felt cold and visibly shivered as they walked into the home.

"Hello, Mrs Warrington. I am Lavonne, we spoke on the phone," he said, addressing Amy. Amy redirected his attentions toward Emily. "I am sorry for your loss," said Lavonne looking critically at Emily. She appeared younger than her twenty-nine years, with no make-up and her hair gathered in a simple ponytail. Too young to be a widow. "We talked about the deluxe package. If you could come into my office, we can discuss this matter further." Emily and Amy followed behind Lavonne into his ornate office. It was burdened with velvet chairs, gold painted lamps, and heavy brocade curtains. "Please be seated." He motioned to Emily and Amy the two chairs in front of his large mahogany desk. Emily noticed a half glass of old water. All she could think was how awful that the water was stagnant and lead to nowhere and was continuously surrounded by death. She chided herself for having such ridiculous thoughts. Emily was acutely brought back to the present.

"Mrs Warrington, I am sure this is an arduous time for you and the rest of Mr Warrington's family. It is my job to make this easier by handling all of the details of the funeral. To start this process, I will need the four thousand dollars. Would you like to pay by check or by card?"

"Oh, by card, I guess," Emily answered absent-mindedly. She grabbed her phone from her purse and typed in her bank user ID and password to transfer the money from her savings to her checking account. She looked at the savings account balance and then looked at it again. She retyped the information at least three times, thinking that there must be some mistake. There was a little over nine thousand dollars in the savings account. They had saved almost thirty-five thousand dollars over the past five years, including the small inheritance from Luke's mom. This was a pittance compared to the debt in student loans, but it was what they had as a nest egg. How could it be almost gone? Panic again rose into her throat.

"Is there a problem, ma'am?"

"Uh, I'm not sure."

"We have already arranged to have Mr Warrington transferred here from the morgue, should I change these plans?" asked Lavonne in a drawn out and mildly patronizing manner.

"No. Uh, we can go ahead," said Emily, still stunned. "We should go with the standard package though," she said quietly.

"I see," said Lavonne. "I will still need three thousand dollars today, so we can proceed as planned and five thousand on the day of the service."

Emily transferred the money and paid with her card. She felt nauseous. She suddenly looked pale and tired.

"Are you okay," asked Amy, her voice conveying her concern.

"I don't know," said Emily. Once in the jeep, Amy asked again if Emily was all right. "Amy, I don't know what's going on. Luke had been fired from his job and didn't even mention it to me, he was supposed to be in Atlanta when he was in the accident, and now almost all of our savings are gone. It just keeps getting worse," said Emily in disbelief.

"Do you need any money?" asked Amy.

"No. Thank you, but no," Emily said politely. "You have been so amazing, Amy. I don't know how I could ever repay you." Hurt transiently moved across Amy's eyes and then the look of concern returned.

"Nothing to repay," said Amy. "Is it okay if I just drop you off? I am on call tomorrow, so I need to get to bed early."

"Of course," replied Emily. "Get your sleep." Not really processing any of the interaction, relying again on social convention.

Emily got out of the jeep and walked up the pavement to the door. Oliver and Rachel were both shouting, "Mommy!"

"Hi, guys. What have you been doing?"

"I played with my toys. I can't wait for my birthday toys," said Oliver hopefully. Rachel was wearing her clear plastic shoes, a pink skirt, and three brightly colored necklaces. It brought a brief smile to Emily's face, observing Rachel's fashion statement. Oliver's birthday. Emily had almost forgot. She had already booked a local venue for the event and ordered food and party favors. A *Paw Patrol* birthday party. It would cost around four hundred dollars with the cake but not including a gift for Oliver. Another thing she would not be able to do. Another disappointment for her children. A funeral and a birthday in the same week. Death was to outshine the celebration of life, in the darkness of this circumstance. Luke would not care, but she had to publicly honor him. To honor his life in front of people who barely knew him and could not care the least about who he is as a person. Was. Emily was no longer certain she knew who he was, this thought brought fresh panic. Emily wished she were brave enough to have a cheap cremation and keep the lavish birthday party.

She looked up and Mrs Lundgren had put on her coat and was ready to leave. "Thank you, Mrs Lundgren, how much do I owe you?"

She seemed embarrassed with the question and averted her gaze. "We'll talk about that at another time, I know you are going through so much right now," said Mrs Lundgren quietly and let herself out.

Emily had sat in the overstuffed chair in the living room for what seemed like an eternity. Frozen in time each thought suspended, unconnected and unprocessed. Emily could see the light fading around her to dusk but was still unable to move. The silence was sharply interrupted by the screams of Oliver; Rachel had hit him over the head with a car. He was crying and Emily was triggered into action to console him when she noticed blood on his shirt, and he was holding his forehead, bright red blood oozing out from under his fingers. All Emily could say was, "Really?" She looked for the wound and found a three to four centimeter linear laceration over the left eyebrow, exuding fresh blood. She grabbed some toilet paper and said for him to hold it on his head while she looked for the first aid kit. Once she found the kit, she cleaned the wound and applied direct pressure, but it was still bleeding. She could see it was fairly deep. It would be a trip to the emergency department. There was no one who could watch Rachel so it appeared they would all be going. D-Three to Four without Luke.

She had Oliver hold the dressing on the wound while she put on his and Rachel's coats. She would have to go in her plastic shoes as Emily did not have the will to fight that battle. The ED seemed relatively quiet. Emily had deliberately gone to the children's hospital to hasten the suturing. This time of year, the wait times were usually tolerable. They knew what to do to get a screaming, almost four year old to comply. He was assessed quickly, the attending recognized Emily and engaged in the usual small talk. Emily said as little as possible. She was just too tired to discuss the mess that was her life.

The wound had been thoroughly cleaned by the nurse and Oliver had been given some Ativan to help calm him down for the procedure. Lidocaine was injected around the wound and four interrupted sutures were expertly placed with good opposition of the wound edges. Oliver was sleepy by the time the procedure was completed. Rachel was initially interested and then got on and off of Emily's lap at least five times. One of the clinical assistants eventually asked if Rachel would like to see the fish. They had a large fish tank in the lobby with brightly colored goldfish.

The young CMA asked if it was, "Okay to take Rachel for a walk to the lobby." Emily thankfully agreed, as did Rachel.

A few minutes later, the assistant brought back a crying Rachel. She was sad because, "The pish was died. Why does Daddy and the pish died?" Emily had to bite her lip to hold back the tears. Rachel ran over to Oliver. "Ollie, Ollie!"

"Honey, Oliver is okay," Emily said as calmly as she could. "He got the owie on his head, but he is okay."

"I gived him the owie," said Rachel plainly.

"Yes, sweetie you gave him the owie. But I know you love Ollie and it was an accident. I know you would never want to hurt him."

"Why so many owies?" said Rachel as she threw her hands in the air dramatically.

"I wish I knew," Emily said. "I wish I knew." She put their coats on and guided both children through the hospital and into the car. They both fell asleep before she left the parking lot. Emily felt drained. She had gone for months with sleep deprivation without feeling so weary. Fortunately, there was little traffic on the streets and they made it home in good time. Once she got home, she put the children in their beds, just removing their coats and shoes. She sat on the couch motionless. The impact of Luke's death and her financial situation hit her hard. She would start to get caught up in the chaos of daily living and their situation could almost be an illusion. It was only when it was quiet that reality would come back in glaring detail. Why was this happening? Emily still could not face sleeping in her bedroom, so she grabbed a blanket and pillow and again fell into a restless sleep on the couch.

The funeral would be in two days. They would have the wake tomorrow. Emily had given the addresses of all of Luke's known living relatives, and the apologies had started to come in both through email and snail mail. A couple of the neighbors had brought casseroles and condolences. Most of whom Emily had seen but had only said a cursory 'hello' or 'good afternoon' or 'nice weather.' Emily was touched and surprised that they seemed to be genuinely sorry for Luke's passing. Luke had apparently been the social one in their relationship.

D-Four to Five post-Luke, Emily would focus on the children and the details of the funeral. The funeral director *extraordinaire*, Lavonne, would take care of the service. Emily would have to use most of what was left of her savings to pay for the food and flowers. She would have to tell herself to 'just get through this' several times per day when the panic would start rising in her chest.

The casket was open at the wake and there was Luke. His face was made up and waxy, his eyes closed. No sign of the injuries sustained, only the made-up version of Luke. She wanted to wipe off the make-up and sanitized vision and show the world the raw violence of his death, of the hole torn through their world. Instead, she gently touched his lips knowing she would never do this again. He had on his favorite blue suit. This was not Luke. Emily felt the pain and then the tears well up in her eyes. She had so many questions that would never be answered.

As Emily looked at him, she whispered, "Who are you? What have you done to us?" Emily looked around at the many people who attended the wake. Some she knew, some she did not, some she could vaguely remember. Oliver and Rachel were being watched by Mrs Lundgren. One day seemed to melt into the next: blending into the night and then into the next amorphous day. Death. People. Fear. Confusion. Routine. The only relief was found in Oliver and Rachel. Their candor and innocence. Their demands did not allow for the indulgence of self-pity.

D-Five post-Luke, the funeral. Emily felt numb. She was the grieving widow, mother to Luke's two young children. Lavonne was expert at giving a moving but concise service. He had done his research. Some of Luke's family were there, many work colleagues, friends, neighbors etc. There were also a couple of guys who Emily was sure she had never met but had been scanning the room full of people, most likely colleagues of Luke's. Emily had thought about having a minister deliver the eulogy, but Luke was not religious, and Emily's faith had laid dormant for years.

The cemetery was small and quiet. The neat rows of headstones sprinkled gingerly with varying shades of dirty grey snow. Lavonne said a few words and then Luke was gone forever. No more to be beheld. No questioning of the changes of his face. The last images of him were witnessed. These would be the visions which would haunt

Emily's dreams forever more. The ill-fitting suit and waxen skin. Emily carried Rachel and held Oliver's hand. They were three. Their world entire wrapped up in one another. Emily held them closer with this knowledge.

Back to the funeral home for more condolences and sustenance. Rachel and Oliver were hiding under the tables. They both seemed bewildered with the process. They were unsettled and were alternating between whining and fighting. Hiding under the table was the calmest they had been during the day. Emily was wavering from stoically accepting condolences and barely holding herself together. Amy had helped throughout the day. She had helped Emily feed Oliver and Rachel and had also played referee more than once. Retreating from the formalities. This looked tempting, but she would eventually grab both of them from under the table and resume the charade. The rest of the funeral passed without an incident.

"Thank you, Lavonne," Emily closed her eyes and whispered. When it was over Emily paid the final bill and gathered the children and headed for home. It was over. Luke's young life. Her life as his wife. Oliver and Rachel as his children. Final.

Day-Seven to Eight, post-Luke. PL. Emily needed to call Ashley; she was in no way ready to go back to work. Emily dialed Ashley's number. Emily heard the familiar high-pitched, strained voice. *"Hello, this is Ashley Larson, I am away from my desk right now, but leave a message and I will get back to you."* Emily was relieved that she did not have to speak to her directly. She left a message that she would need at least another week to sort out her affairs related to Luke's death. Emily did not believe in saying euphemisms for death. It seemed dishonest and minimized the magnitude of the reality. Death caused despair. Death caused pain. Death caused destruction. Death separated families. Death was the finale. Someone does not 'pass', they were dead, lost to us. No more. To say 'pass' indicates that they are going on to some journey, like moving to a new house or a new career. Emily had once thought about death in this way, but that was a long time ago and before her husband died. The cold lifeless body does not look as though it was in transition. It looked like the end. Emily felt a cold lump in her stomach and a feeling of dread wash over her. She could face this, but not with arbitrary euphemisms. Death was death.

Chapter 10
Moving Forward and Birthdays

Day-Nine post-Luke. PL. It was over and also just beginning. Gone was the husband and father, the intact family. What was left was the broken trio. The widow. The fatherless. Even the time before was a facade. Innocence was another casualty of the last week and a half. Amazing how life can change completely in such a short time. Emily woke up to the noise created by Oliver and Rachel. They were making cereal. Milk was all over the table and the floor. That will teach me to let them get up first, thought Emily. She cleaned up the mess and made a cup of coffee. There was a flatness to everything. The house seemed empty and comfortless. Food didn't have a taste. He was gone. Emily would need to remind herself over and over so that it would sink in each day. It was the kids and Emily in their new world.

She had to think about how she was going to support her family on a resident's salary. She did not have long to do, only a matter of weeks, but it would take months before she was credentialed and employed at her attending job. She was fortunate that at least she had an offer of a job. She would need to go back after this week.

The hospital seemed like a distant memory, a faint shadow of her former life.

How could they be in this position? What made Luke spend their savings, their small nest egg? Their barrier from catastrophe. How could he be so selfish? She missed him and was angry with him for leaving them. Especially without any protection. Where did the money go? Why did he leave his job? She needed to know what was so enticing that he left them destitute and alone. She entered his office with trepidation. His papers still strewn over his desk, last handled by Luke. The hope that he would organize them at a later date. His smell still lingering. Emily knew this is where she needed to start.

She looked through the papers on his desk first. She organized them into dates and then into subject matter. Most of the papers were at least three months old. They were related to some of his larger clients, like Petfoods, or working on other nameless corporate contracts. Endless number crunching. From first glance nothing seemed out of order. Luke liked to double-check the figures from computing programs manually. Emily noticed that the spreadsheets had become more erratic and incomplete over the past three months.

She looked at the savings account for withdrawals in an effort to piece together the events that lead to Luke losing his job and spending their reserve. There were several withdrawals two to three weeks apart. The amounts varied from two hundred to fifteen hundred dollars and all were withdrawn in person. With each withdrawal the meagre nest egg was progressively unraveled, until there remained the paltry amount that would barely cover Oliver's birthday party. Emily scoured every withdrawal to see if there were a name or some evidence of the story behind these actions. Something that would explain why Luke betrayed his family.

Emily could hear Oliver coming downstairs and calling out to her. She got up and closed the door to his office. She had only begun the search through the pieces that had been Luke's separate life. Emily would now need to plan Oliver's birthday and still pay the utilities next week, pay the mortgage, pay Mrs Lundgren etc. Life moves on.

The birthday party would need to be at home. The extensive list of friends and neighbors would be whittled to a few friends and their parents. The list derived mostly from preschool and their neighborhood. Emily would make the cake. It could not be that hard, right? Emily could make a basic meal, which was healthy and palatable, but she had not baked since she was a teenager. It would be a challenge. She would look up the *Paw Patrol* characters; Oliver was partial to Chase or Marshall. *Paw Patrol*, the action-packed series with cute puppies as the protagonists. Emily trawled the Internet for ideas and then set off with Rachel and Oliver to the store for ingredients: sugar, flour, food coloring, eggs, baking powder etc. Emily printed off images of the characters and then traced them and painted and colored the figures, whilst Oliver and Rachel were in bed. She was thankful for the distraction. Her heart was heavy but at least she could keep her hands busy. She created a small station made out of cardboard and several bowls that she decorated with paw prints; she would make a cake in the shape of a dog bone. Tomorrow she would go to the dollar store or local discount store to get the helmets. It had taken every ounce of her will just to get up in the morning. She would spend most of the night pacing and worrying how or if they would ever move forward. There were nights when she was violently gripped with panic and would hyperventilate until she would feel herself nearly losing consciousness. Despite the weariness that had begun to settle into her bones, she would do this party for Oliver.

Oliver had become increasingly excited about his birthday. Emily had bought the balloons in primary colors and the brightly colored pictures had been cut out and placed throughout the house. Emily had bought premade pastry and cut out bones decorated with the *Paw Patrol* character names. She had streamers in blue and yellow crisscrossing the ceiling. Emily had made the name tags and placed them on the decorated table. She made punch and little sandwiches, well regular sandwiches cut into four parts, with the crusts removed. There were bowls of snack foods that she would not normally let them eat. Emily looked around the house and it looked like a birthday party was about to happen. Soon the children would be arriving for the party. There were four children from the area and three from his preschool. Most of the children would be accompanied by their mothers and one child attending with his father. Oliver and Rachel were both so excited. Emily looked over at Oliver. He was sitting at the table, looking out of the window. Oliver appeared unexpectedly sad in the midst all of the preparations.

"What's wrong Oliver?" Emily asked.

"I thought my birthday would be the best, but I miss Daddy so much."

"I know, buddy, we all do," was all Emily could muster. Sometimes, the pain would come back fresh and brutal. She could mostly force herself not to be overwhelmed during the day, but the sadness of Oliver in the midst of the colorful chaos, had caught her off guard. No time to steel herself to get through the moment. She would have to work on this response once today was over.

Emily baked the cakes the day before, to make them easier to manipulate into their desired shapes. One rectangular cake and two round cakes cut in half to create a bone. It seemed fairly straightforward. However, part of one of the round cakes stuck to the pan and was crumbling, so she could only use a small portion of the cake. There was no time to make a new cake so she arranged the cakes as best she could and added copious amounts of white frosting. She tried to smooth the frosting into a semblance of a bone. She had put a pink line horizontally at the ends of the rectangle to create some definition. She put candles on the cake and licorice for the letters. She could get 'Happy B'day Ollie,' on the cake, the 'Ollie' extended onto one of the round cakes. She was hoping the lit candles would distract the children from the misshapen slabs. At least the ice cream would be okay as it was store bought. The guests were punctual in arriving to the party. Shoes and coats cluttering the small entrance of the house. Presents were strewn over the decorated kitchen table spilling onto the floor. The parents awkwardly stood by the front door, some expressed sympathy for her loss and others avoided eye contact altogether. Emily invited them in, and some parents left their children whilst others monitored their children with the intense surveillance of a navy seal. Emily had worked through the games and food far too quickly and some arguing ensued as to what games they wanted to play next and the rules of the games. Oliver thought he should be the game master as it was his birthday, some of the bossier kids fiercely objected as, "Just because it's your birthday, it doesn't mean you're the boss of everything". Emily played peacemaker on several occasions to soothe the rankled tempers. The badges were a particularly bad idea as they crumbled as soon as a child tried to put them on. The children seemed to be enjoying themselves despite the imperfections of the day. This is why Emily loved children. They were generally honest and forgiving.

It was time for the cake. One of the children asked Oliver, what kind of a cake he was having. He replied that it was a bone for *Paw Patrol*. "It doesn't look like a bone," said Sarah looking quizzically, tossing her blonde curls as she shook her head.

One of the other children chimed in. "Yeah that isn't like any bone that I've seen."

Another child, said, "It looks like a widgy." He clarified that a 'widgy' was another name for his penis and 'testamentacles'. The children all agreed that that was what the cake resembled.

Oliver started to get upset. "It isn't a widgy, it is a bone," he cried. Rachel started to cry in support for Oliver. Emily started singing 'Happy Birthday' before it got too ugly. The candles were lit and blown out and then Emily abruptly cut the cake. This silenced the critics. Emily was rethinking the liking children thing. The rest of the party went fairly smoothly. Oliver received several presents consisting of cars, trucks, diggers and *Paw Patrol* characters. The guests left as expeditiously as they arrived, and the house looked very much like a children's party had just taken place. Emily made a cup of coffee and let Rachel and Oliver play on the floor with his new toys. He only reluctantly agreed to allow her to play with his toys and then only the ones he did not like very much. Toys such as unpopular *Paw Patrol* characters or single Matchbox cars with broken doors. She was happy to be playing with Oliver in any form.

Oliver looked at Emily and said, "Thank you, Mommy, for my birthday, but next year you should buy the cake." She smiled and nodded in agreement. Emily pulled their pajamas from the drier and ran a bath for the children. They were both pretty grubby from the day's events. Emily placed both children into the bath and did her best to wash their hair despite their protestations. When they were sufficiently wrinkly, she wrapped each child in a warm towel. Oliver put on his own pajamas and Emily dressed Rachel. Oliver slowly walked into his room.

He looked at Emily and asked, "Mommy since this is my birthday can I sleep in your bed?"

"Of course, Oliver, you can always sleep in my bed." Emily was surprised as Oliver had slept in his own bed since he was a year and a half, and he rarely slept with Luke and Emily. Even when he woke up with a bad dream he would come in their room for a while and then return to his own bed. Rachel added that she too would sleep in Mommy's bed in honor of Ollie's birthday. Oliver and Rachel got into the bed and Emily tucked them in and Oliver selected his favorite book to read. Emily had to go into Oliver's room to get the book and by the time she returned, they were both asleep. Emily looked around at the mess to clean up. The crumpled chaos echoing the state of her mind.

Chapter 11
Real Life as a Single Parent

D-Thirteen to Fourteen post-Luke. Emily's time off was almost up. The raw effects of Luke's death were acutely felt. Emily mustered the strength to call Ashley. "Hello Ashley, it's Emily Warrington." Emily was about to leave a voice mail when Ashley picked up the phone.

"Hello, Emily, how have you been? It must be tough without Luke," Ashley said in her usual high-pitched voice.

"Okay, I think, I am just trying to make sense out of it all," Emily said quietly. It still didn't feel real.

"You realize that you need to come back to work by Monday or you will not be able to complete your residency in time to take over as attending," said Ashley in the same high-pitched pseudo-concerned tone.

"I know, Ashley, but I need to figure things out with the kids, the house, and the money..."

After a long pause, Ashley responded with, "You have until Wednesday next week, one week from today. Any longer and you're out of the residency for the year, maybe permanently." In an uncustomary low and metered voice she said, "I would hate for you to miss out on the attending job from Dr Meyer, not everyone gets such a lucky break, toodles." Ashley had reverted back to her high-pitched twang. Emily's disdain for Ashley was renewed every time they spoke. Her condescending, thinly veiled contempt for anyone who was not her was clearly evident. The sickly sugar-coated packaging completed the effect. She hung up feeling both spent and relieved that she would have a few more days to think things through. This was not going to be a good day. The weight of the responsibility was crushing like an anvil on her chest. Her time was running out to pick up the fragments of their lives and make something recognizable again. She knew that she needed to arrange care for Oliver and Rachel, but she just sat on the floor staring at a blank wall.

Emily took care of the children and methodically fed them and absent-mindedly listened to their complaints and stories. She could not stop thinking about what was going to happen in a week. How she would pay for everything, including childcare and then the mortgage. Her meagre resident salary would not begin to cover their expenses. Their residue of savings was further dried up with the funeral and living expenses. They were broke. If they could get through the next few months things would turn around. Emily could make enough to catch up their bills. However, she needed to get through this time. She made an extensive list of what she could do to save money and how to scrape by with expenses. Her growing up in poverty had trained her well for this eventuality. She could feel her mind switch over into autopilot in the process. She would apply for fuel assistance and talk to the bank and the mortgage company; she would talk to

ECFE about Oliver and publicly funded preschool programs. She would make casseroles and chilis despite the children's protests. She would walk to where she could and bring her lunches. She would see about a loan until she could take up her attending position. She would contact student loans for a suspension of her loans based on personal hardship. She would talk to Mrs Lundgren regarding partial payments for a few months. She knew these were all long shots, but she would try as she was in full on paucity mode. She learned this position well whilst growing up. She had to protect her family and to provide for them. She would go through Luke's papers to see if she could recoup any of the money spent or withdrawn from their accounts. She was dreading this last part of the plan the most. She wanted to know but was afraid of what she might uncover. She had already been through too many changes and traumas over the past two weeks, she was not sure of her resolve with further revelations. She could not go back to the tired but happyish resident with a family. The one with a husband who had to bear too much of the burden of their mutual choices and their beautiful children. Even though he was not perfect, he loved his children. He loved them in a way that only a parent could love. An intricate love. One with joy, compassion, sacrifice, protectiveness, fatigue, disappointment, fear, hope, guilt and pride all coalescing in varying quantities depending on the specific moment. Emily was now everything to her children. Breadwinner and caretaker, maid and cook. Chauffeur. Coach. Defender. And too many other things to recite. Emily felt weary just recounting these responsibilities. She had them before, but she could share them with Luke. He was tired but did not seem to mind. He had been so brave letting his career take the back seat so Emily could fulfil her dream. Spousal love was also complicated. Maybe all love was, she just hadn't noticed. Her gut wrenched in need for that complicated love. To talk to him. To ask questions and really listen to his responses. To see him. To smell his hair. To feel his touch once again. She would not pull away this time or let him pull away. She felt as though she was going mad. She was so angry with Luke one minute and then having a blinding need for him the next. Sometimes she would cry and sometimes she would sit numb for minutes to hours. At least she hid most of this from Oliver and Rachel. It had only been two weeks. Emily envied women who had family to take care of life while they grieved. How they could self-indulgently stay in their bedroom for days or weeks. To have someone bring you food and watch your children. To cocoon your grief until a catharsis was reached. Not to have to think about the mundane and necessary. Paying the bills, working, providing the support, being strong. Figuring out how life would now have to be lived. Making it up minute to minute. Feeling paralyzed by the fear and dread. She was thankful for Amy and Mrs Lundgren. Their kindness and support. Oliver and Rachel had made the journey bearable. They were her journey. She was grateful for the busyness of her life when she was thinking coherently again. The waves of self-pity would wash over her without warning. She had little defense and could be easily swept away with the anguish and precariousness of their predicament. Emily was desperately trying to find an anchor, so she could be their anchor. She would figure this out too.

Day-? Post-Luke, Emily was not counting the days any longer. She was just trying to tread water. Emily was fortunately able to defer her student loans. The bank manager would consider a loan but was doubtful in view of her colossal student loans and her current low paying position as a resident. Emily enlisted Amy to watch the kids while she worked through her poverty survival list. She walked up the steps to Mrs Lundgren's house with trepidation. Mrs Lundgren saw Emily coming up to the door and opened it before Emily could knock.

"Hello, Mrs Lundgren, could I come in?" Emily said hopefully.

"Of course," said Mrs Lundgren. Mrs Lundgren showed Emily into her modest living room and gestured for Emily to sit down. "How have you been faring?" she asked.

"I am just making it through each day," said Emily flatly.

"How can I help?" asked Mrs Lundgren.

"I know you have already helped me out with the children, above and beyond the call of duty, but I need to ask for more." Without taking a full breath Emily continued. "Could you watch the children and get half of the amount that I owe you until I get my attending position? I know this is unfair," Emily added, "but I don't know what else to do. I have to go back to work next week or I will not be able to finish my residency on time. I would lose any chance at an attending position for the foreseeable future. With all of our debt, I don't know how we would make it through financially. I would have to make up the time and also additional time for the rotation. If not, I would have no job. No one will hire you without completion of a residency…"

Mrs Lundgren looked away. She took what seemed an eternity before she answered. "Emily, I haven't been paid for at least two months. I also have a rather uncertain position. Abby has continued to urge me to watch the children. You know how fond I am of both of them and this was also a large part of looking after them despite the lack of compensation. However, Abby is moving back to North Carolina and I am going with her." Mrs Lundgren could not hide the fact that she was visibly upset. Unshed tears welled up in her pale blue eyes. "Abby has made some rather unsavory friends and it would be better for everyone if we moved away. Abby has also started using again and she cannot care for herself right now. I am really very sorry, Emily."

Despite her own need, Emily felt a pang of sympathy for Mrs Lundgren. She had a difficult and painful road ahead of her. A road she had traveled many times before. There had been progress at times, strengthening the glimmers of hope. However, there were many more setbacks, each time taking its toll. Until even the progress is met with stone. "Emily, Abby is also grieving." Mrs Lundgren looked at Emily directly in the eyes. "Abby and

Luke had become very close over the past couple of months."

"What do you mean?" said Emily trying to steady her voice.

Mrs Lundgren looked at an invisible speck on the floor. "Oh, just that they had become friends."

"Is that all they were?" Emily snapped. "Look, Mrs Lundgren, if you know more than you are telling me, I would appreciate the truth. I have had to decipher too many things already."

"I know, Emily, I don't know why I even mentioned it," said Mrs Lundgren quietly. "Just be careful, you don't always know who those closest to you really are."

Before Emily could ask any further, Mrs Lundgren had got up and directed her towards the door. Emily followed her and left, feeling confused and nauseous. Despite her bewilderment, the panic over how she was going to take care of the children took precedence. Emily was still trying to process the information and emotions when she arrived home. Once in the driveway she sat in the car trying to regain her composure and to rethink her poverty survival plan. It was little more than two weeks since Luke's death and she felt at least twenty years older. She could see Oliver looking out of the window and smiling. The weariness would have to wait.

"Hi, Oliver," said Emily waving. Both kids ran to greet her at the door. She barely took her coat off and they were hugging her. There seemed to be an increased intensity as if they sensed the fragility of their situation. More changes were coming. At that moment Emily also clung to them, closing her eyes and feeling the warmth of their small bodies. Soon they were both wriggling to get away.

"Mommy, Rachel broke my fort."

"Ollie not sharing," shouted Rachel in her defense.

"Sorry about the mess," added Amy looking apologetic, coming into the living room. Emily could see that there really had been destruction of a fort in the room. Several blankets and pillows were on the floor littered with crumbs, cars and Lego. Emily could also make out a couple of Cheetos crushed into the carpet.

"Don't worry about it, thanks for watching the kids. It does look like they had fun," said Emily still scanning the room.

"Is she going to watch the kids?" asked Amy while she was digging in her purse for her car keys.

"No, she's moving to North Carolina," said Emily flatly.

"What are you going to do?" asked Amy with uneasiness.

"I don't know. I don't know," said Emily. "On the bright side I have a week to figure this out."

"Oh Emily. Is there anything I can do to help?" asked Amy. Emily knew that Amy was pretty much maxed out with her ability to help. She also worked full-time and had to sort out her own interviews for attending positions. She was currently going through the final details of her own divorce and was still licking her wounds.

"Thanks Amy, for all of your help, I will let you know if I need anything." Amy grabbed her coat and bag and headed out the door to her car. The decrepit jeep disappearing into the grey milieu of the suburban landscape. "Bye, Amy," was all Emily could muster.

One week.

Chapter 12
Lies and Deception

D-too many, post-Luke. It was not even a full three weeks but nothing in her life was the same. Emily would look at happy couples or families and think, hold on to those moments because your lives could change on a dime. Emily knew that she was better off than most as she had the prospect of an illustrious career. She was early in her profession, but she could expect an adequate salary to cover their living expenses and even some luxuries. She could take care of her family. Eventually. She could not imagine how tough it would be to be a single parent without this hope. She felt a wave of compassion towards her mother. It must have been hard, being alone and poor. To be in a small town with few opportunities and fewer friends. To barely make it from one paycheck to the next. Life being so stark and tenuous. Emily had not thought about her mother for several months and then it was only fleeting. The last time was when she received her annual Christmas card. Emily threw the card aside and had not taken the time to read the accompanied letter. Emily had closed the door on that life and living separate made it a cleaner existence. No loose ends. No reminders of her own vulnerability and pain. Her wounds she had meticulously bandaged so they would not bleed onto her new life. The life where she is a respected doctor. A mother and a wife. A life where she would make the decisions about who would or would not be part of her life. A life where she could keep her children safe from disillusionment. Emily felt a fraud knowing she had failed to keep them from disappointment. They had already been through so much in the past few weeks. She had not been able protect them from death. And now she did not know how she would care for them, so she could keep a roof over their heads. She shook her head. She would not fail them.

She would regroup and would see if there were any county operated centers, this might buy her some time. She was not sure of the income requirements. She had concluded that their only asset was the house. She would have to sell it and rent a cheap apartment until she finished her residency. Emily felt somewhat reassured that, even though they would have to move, they could hold the course. Emily would call the real estate agent in the morning. Oliver and Rachel were ready for bed and playing with Oliver's cars on the floor. Emily, silently thanked Amy again for her help.

"Okay guys, time for bed."

"Mommy, can Rachel and me sleep with you? She gets scared at night."

"What do think she is scared of?" asked Emily.

"Noises."

"What noises?" Emily asked.

"House noises," said Oliver trying hard to convey his perspective.

"Are they new noises?" asked Emily.

"I don't know, I just didn't hear them much before."

Emily could hear the furnace switching on. It may be spring, but it was still heating weather. "Is that a 'house' sound?"

"Yep, one of 'em," said Oliver satisfied that he had made his point.

Rachel was reaching for Emily. Emily picked her up and held her in her lap. Rachel looked up at Emily and said, "No work. Mommy home!"

"For now, baby girl," Emily said quietly. "You can both sleep with me, anytime. Even without 'house' noises." They seemed satisfied with that answer and both crawled into Emily's bed. She felt safer having them with her, she could be sure they were secure. Their restless bodies moved around the bed, creating varying configurations throughout the night. Emily was far from rested when she got up in the morning.

She looked up the most popular real estate company on a local web search.

"Hello 'Realtors are Us'. How can I help you?" Emily was transferred to a local agent and then discussed the plans for a quick sale. The agent, David, would come around tomorrow to take photographs and draw up contracts. Emily only had five days left. She could feel her panic rising. Emily tried several daycares, including the local early childhood family education centers. Her income was either too high or they were too expensive and wanted the first and last week's money upfront for both children. Or they were full with waiting lists. Emily just needed more time. Her time off from work had already exceeded the good will of the program. Emily felt sick with her dwindling options. She would beg Mrs Lundgren for the next week just to give her more time. All of the threads Emily thought were in place were unraveling fast. How could he do this to them.

"You bastard!" "You selfish bastard!" she screamed, hurling her mug across the kitchen. The cup shattering into hundreds of pieces and the liquid creating a caramel abstract over the wall. Oliver came running into the kitchen.

"Mommy, Mommy what happened?"

"Oh, I accidently spilled my coffee and dropped my cup. But everything is okay, so don't worry," said Emily in the most comforting voice she could muster.

"It sounded like you threw the cup and were mad at Daddy," Oliver said sheepishly.

"It's okay, Oliver. I'm okay. I did throw the cup, which was not a great choice, but I'm over it now. I am just frustrated and hurting right now. Let me tuck you back into my bed before Rachel gets up."

"Could we have a snack, only just us?" asked Oliver hopefully.

"Sure. What do you want? We have fruit or chips?"

"A sandwich," replied Oliver excitedly. Emily smiled. She made two almond butter and jelly sandwiches. Oliver tolerated tree nuts but could not have peanuts. Emily had become quite fond of almond butter, the salty sweet grittiness. She poured two glasses of milk and brought them into the living room on the coffee table. Oliver seemed satisfied with the arrangement. He ate his sandwich eagerly, getting the jelly over his fingers as he squeezed the bread. "Mommy, thanks for the snack. Can we do this every night? I feel not as sad."

"Probably not at this time every night, but we can always have time together," said Emily, hoping she was handling this in the best way. She never knew whether she should have better answers, to not to yell or throw her mug. To know how to take care of them. She could advise parents of patients, but she was too close to this situation and too raw. She would always fall back on the truth. After Emily and Oliver finished their sandwiches and drank their milk, she picked him up and brought him to her bed. The three of them rapidly developing a familiar sleeping arrangement, each nestled into one another providing warmth and comfort. Emily felt restless tonight, even more than usual. She had not slept well since Luke died. She got up and sat on the couch in the living room with the lamp dimly lit. She was still in disbelief that he was not coming home. Sometimes when the pain would get too much, she would pretend he was away on business and would be home in a few days. Emily felt as though she was free falling most days. Free falling with two small children. Emily had not really appreciated the loneliness of being a single parent. All choices rest on your head. Here she was making it up as she went along. The time of predictability and a well-planned future was over. She would have to summon the strength to move forward another day to hold on to the strands of their lives.

When Emily woke up, she was still in a sitting position on the couch. She pulled the throw blanket from the back of the couch onto her shoulders. She made her way back into to her bedroom and watched Oliver and Rachel asleep so peacefully. Their beautiful faces content for the moment. They had absolute trust in Emily to maintain the stability of their lives. Emily looked at the clock, it was five thirty a.m. This was the start of T minus four days to get Oliver and Rachel care so she could go back to work.

Emily tried to go back to sleep but could not. She got up and wrote out her list once again of all of the things she needed to do to have her family survive. She showered and turned on morning TV for background noise. She glanced at herself in the mirror. She had lost at least ten pounds and had dark circles under her eyes. Her face reflected the pain of the previous weeks. She looked worn from fatigue and grief. Emily knew she would have to remind herself to eat regularly. She needed her strength to manage their new lives. Despite Mrs Lundgren's difficulties, she would keep the children safe.

She woke the children up around seven-thirty. She knew that Mrs Lundgren would be up, she always was an early riser. She dressed the children and hastily put them in their car seats. They would have to come with her to Sarah's house. She hoped this would also help her cause. She knocked on the door and was about to leave when Mrs Lundgren opened the door.

"Come in Emily and Ollie and Miss Rachel. I will get you some oatmeal cookies that I made yesterday and some milk," she said with a smile.

"Mrs Lundgren, could I speak with you privately?"

"Okay, Emily."

"I know you are moving away and have a ton of things to do, but I don't know what to do with Oliver and Rachel. I have four days to find childcare and I don't get paid until next week. If I do not return to work, I will be unable to complete my residency and will have to forfeit my attending job. I know this is not your problem. But if you could help for a week or two so I can figure this mess out. I would be forever grateful and will pay you for everything when I sell the house or start the attending position."

Emily looked away as she could not bear the silence. Her face flushed with the shame of such blatant need. Her insides churning. "I could do maybe one week before it would become too difficult with moving. I am sorry I can't offer more right now. Have you spoken to your mother?", Mrs Lundgren added tentatively.

Emily was taken aback; she hadn't thought about her mother until recently and then was reminded of her twice in the past week. "No, I haven't spoken to her." Emily was grateful for this extra time. She also confirmed with Mrs Lundgren that Abby would be clean. Emily knew this was far from ideal, but she was desperate, and Mrs Lundgren would keep them safe. She was the closest they had to a grandmother. Emily kept telling herself these statements. She grabbed both children and walked towards the door. "Thank you for this time, for your generosity," Emily said, looking Mrs Lundgren in the eye before opening the door. Emily knew this was temporary, but felt relief.

She needed to get home before the real estate agent to tidy up for the photographs. Emily lifted both children from their car seats and brought them into the house. "Rachel and Oliver, you guys need to play in Ollie's room while Mommy cleans up okay?"

"Mommy does Rachel have to come into my room?" said Oliver in protest.

"Yep, she does."

Emily had only begun to pick up toys and vacuuming in the living room when the estate agent knocked on the door. The estate agent was dressed in smart casual clothing and was probably in his early thirties. He extended his hand.

"Hi, I'm David we spoke on the phone yesterday."

"Yes, of course, nice to meet you."

"Are you the owner?" he asked.

"Yes, I am a recent widow, and I can no longer afford the house," Emily blurted out.

"Oh, I see," he said, however, Emily was certain he had no idea. Emily gave him the tour while he would say 'Um' or 'Un huh'. Finally, he had seen the entire house, three bedrooms and three bathrooms, a kitchen, dining room, family room and office. He sat down at the kitchen table and pulled out his papers and placed them on the table. "So, I pulled a search on this property, the value is two hundred and eighty to two hundred and ninety-five thousand dollars in this market. You owe around two hundred and thirty thousand dollars on your first mortgage and thirty thousand on your second mortgage," he added.

"What second mortgage?" said Emily in disbelief. "There must be some mistake." But she had been through enough over the previous three weeks to know that it wasn't. "I would have had to sign before there could be a second mortgage and I certainly wouldn't have agreed and jeopardize our home. What is the mortgage company?" He gave her all of the information that he had. Century mortgage with the mortgage amount and with a current status: sixty days late. Emily's heart started to race. Another bomb dropped. She had to take a few deep breaths before she could trust her voice again. "I will call the mortgage company, it's illegal! I never agreed to this. You can't get a mortgage on a joint property with only one signature." Emily almost screamed.

"Good luck, ma'am," said David. "Did you still want to proceed with the sale?"

"Ah, yes," she said mumbled.

She contacted the mortgage company, and they had her signature on the mortgage. She did explain that her signature was either a forgery or obtained without explicit understanding of the purpose. She had not agreed to the second mortgage. They said that they would look into this but that this was unlikely to change her situation as they did not have any evidence that it wasn't her who signed the forms and the money had been released several months ago. If the mortgage had been in good standing, it would help, but as it was there was little hope that they would reverse their decision.

If she could sell the house, she could maybe make fifteen thousand dollars after everything was paid up. She really had no alternative. She would have try and manage the house payments in the meantime. One more thing when she did not think she could handle 'one more thing'. It is amazing how we say this phrase when we really have no idea what we can handle and what will cause us to break. That last straw. Emily was reflecting on Luke. He seemed to be okay and to be able to take care of his mother and watch her die while caring for two young children. But he broke somewhere along the way. Maybe he was broken much earlier but had constructed a veneer as an illusion. Sometimes we never know. Do we know anyone? Emily could not go down this path of indulgent self-pity. At least not now. She was frightened but her role as mother and protector had never been more defined. Her children would be taken care of for another week. And Emily would work at getting them into a more permanent placement. The house was now officially on the market. Emily didn't feel anything about having to sell the house. It had become a reminder of the sham that was their lives. Their misguided hopes and dreams. The pain of the recent events was now an integral part of the structure of the house. No. She would not mourn the loss of their home.

Chapter 13
New Routines in the Hospital

Emily called the clinic to find out where she was needed the following week. She spoke to the coordinator for that site, Mary. She was a warm woman who was larger than life, she had fiery artificially colored hair and broad features. She told Emily how sorry she was for her loss and Emily was touched by her sincerity. Mary explained that she would be with Doctor Jessup the next week as the other attendings already had residents. Emily groaned audibly. He was known to be a difficult attending. He was pedantic and uninspiring. He would focus on the minutia and miss the diagnosis. Doctor Jessup was known to have the residents carry out his scut work and would blame any of his own insufficiencies on the said resident. Needless to say, he was unpopular. Unlike Doctor Meyer, he was wholly unobservant and preferred sycophants to competence. Emily knew she was in trouble. She would have to practice sounding genuine with her admiration. It was distasteful at best, but she would have to figure a way to finish her residency, so they could move forward. She would have to think of Oliver and Rachel. Emily could do this. It was a minor thing considering all of the other challenges that her family had faced over the past few weeks.

It is amazing how life continues to evolve only to settle into new routines. Emily had managed to get the children cared for, for another week and the house on the market and a plan to return to work. It was a start. She still needed longer term plans and money to survive until the house was sold. The truth would have to wait until she was sure of their survival. Emily was not sure she could even process the truth right now. Her brain wanted to shut down.

"Oliver and Rachel, come on. Let's go to the park." They both came running into the kitchen.

"Yeah park!" shouted Rachel. Emily put on their boots and coats and bundled them into the car. There was still slushy snow on the ground and mud underneath. Emily jumped over a puddle and on to a swing. She helped Oliver onto a swing and then pushed him until his small legs were able to take over. She picked Rachel up and sat with her on the next swing. She held her on her lap and extended and flexed her legs and they flew higher while Emily pulled Rachel closer. Rachel giggled and then settled into Emily as they rose and fell. Emily felt free for a few moments. She had not been on a swing in years and it felt good. She was aware of how it may have looked, the three of them swinging over the snow. They were the only people at the park, but she didn't care if it had been full of people. The playground just emerging from under the blanket of white. Remnants of the snow remaining as splotches of white or grey patches haphazardly strewn over the equipment. Emily grabbed both of the children and carried them over to the slide. Oliver climbed up the ladder and slid down and into a puddle. He got up and started to cry because he was wet. Emily picked him up and found another puddle and started to jump in it. Oliver momentarily was stunned watching Emily and feeling the splash of water. A few seconds later, Oliver and Rachel wriggled to get down and also jumped up and down causing the icy water to soak their clothes and spatter their faces. They started to laugh as they jumped faster and faster. Eventually they fell down into the chilly water. Emily hugged them both and decided it was time to go and get them warm. It had been a long time since they had laughed together. She buckled them into their car seats and drove home. Oliver and Rachel had fallen asleep soon after they drove off. Emily thought she may be losing it, but her children did not seem to notice, or to care. They embraced the spontaneous Emily. She would have to resume the ordered and routine Emily in a few days. Emily had always looked forward to going back to work, but not now. She felt a sense of dread. It was too soon, and she was too raw. She needed to be with Oliver and Rachel until their brains managed to grasp their new existence. Until they got to know who they were as a family. Emily reminded herself of her responsibilities and that she needed to provide for her children.

The phone ringing interrupted her thoughts. An unknown number. She declined the call but was annoyed that these unknown calls were occurring at least twice daily. Her number must be on some caller list. Her mind went back to her family. Emily felt tired but she knew that they were still more fortunate than many families that she had seen or patients she had treated. She tried to focus on what was still right with their lives, but some days it was harder than others

Emily knew she needed to get the house ready for sale. She would have to repaint the kids' bathroom and deep clean the house. Luke had done most of the repairs and painting when it was needed. Emily had helped, but mostly it was a show of support rather than actual help. Another change she would need to get used to. Each change piled onto the last; creating barriers that seemed insurmountable and a vision that was unrecognizable. She felt awe at how single parents do this day in and day out. How they manage everything. The finances, the housework, the well-being of their children, and countless other tasks which were too exhausting even to contemplate. And the loneliness. At least she had started to work through the tasks, to move forward on this path.

Chapter 14
Iris and Dr Jessop

Going back to work. This day had arrived far too quickly. Emily still felt in disarray and her life in chaos, but she had to move forward. Her family depended on it. Emily had not slept well the night before. Rachel and Oliver had taken their usual places in her bed. The three of them entangled, safe within the confines of their little island. Emily had laid out their clothes the night before. She felt uneasy as if she had never left her children to go to work before. But that was in her other life. The facade of a happy life. A life when she was not the sole carer of her children. A life where the responsibility was parceled out in neat packages among two parents and a babysitter. A life where bad things did not happen to their family. That life was over, and Emily knew it. She would have to forge a new path for them to survive. It was all uncharted territory.

By the time morning came, Emily had been awake for most of the night. She was thinking about the plan of action in the morning and apprehension at leaving her children and returning to medicine. A distant memory wrapped up in her other life. The alarm sounded far too quickly. It had seemed that she had just closed her eyes and the loud bell-like chime was sounding. Emily looked at the clock. It was six a.m. on the dot. She moved Rachel off of her and headed for the bathroom. She stumbled into the shower and felt the warm water wash over her. It was both comforting and sobering. She grabbed her towel and picked up her clothes from the chair which had been laid out the night before. She called out to Rachel and Oliver to get up. She dressed Rachel while Oliver was still lying in the bed. Emily thought there would be less acrimony regarding the clothing selection this way. Rachel groaned here and there but was mostly compliant. Oliver was fairly cooperative but asked so many questions that Emily's brain was tired before the day was actually started.

"Mommy why are we up? Mommy why are you dressed like that?"

"Like what?" Emily responded.

"Like a grown up," said Oliver in a slightly frustrated manner. The questions seemed never-ending. Emily went into the kitchen ignoring the rest of the interrogation. She threw a K cup into the Keurig and three slices of bread into the toaster. She pulled out two kids' yogurts from the refrigerator. Everything was going fairly well, so far at least. She tried to feed Rachel, but Rachel kept pursing her lips and spitting out what yogurt had made it into her mouth. Rachel usually fed herself, but they did not have time for her dawdling today. Mercifully, Oliver ate his yogurt without complaint. Emily washed their faces and brushed their teeth as best she could in the mad rush that was the morning. She bundled them into their car seats.

She reached Mrs Lundgren's house in good time. Oliver and Rachel were happy to see Mrs Lundgren but Rachel would not let go of Emily's hand. When Emily would pry her off one hand she would grab onto the other hand. Mrs Lundgren eventually reached out to Rachel and pulled her away from Emily.

"Mommy we go home," cried Rachel. Emily thanked Mrs Lundgren and hurried to get into her car. The new clinic was not much further in distance from the hospital but was located in a more central location, which caused traffic to almost stand still at least twice a day. Emily could feel the tension rise when she looked at the time. She missed her turn off as she could not get over fast enough. Damn, another five minutes wasted. She maneuvered around several vehicles and brightly colored dumpsters to get to the clinic entrance. She hurried into the clinic, already late. The clinic looked clearly worn. The out-of-date pictures accompanied the sirocco sconces and the carpet faded where stains had been removed. The lights too bright and unnatural. Emily was home. This was the kind of place that welcomed residents. They were cheap labor and most of the patients did not seem to mind repeating their histories and waiting for their appointments. By and large, the patients were tolerant with their doctors in training. The bemused histories and fumbled examinations. They gained personal attention and their chance to be heard. Private clinics did not have the tolerance for patients without insurance or those who were meandering historians, taking up costly time. Those who were more fragmented. They were the magnanimous teachers of these junior doctors, many of the doctors would eventually graduate to private clinics. The clinics where money played a much greater role, and the doctor would become secondary to the administrative business drones. The years of training to gain knowledge and its application only to be diminished by those with their newly minted MBAs in finance. In training, idealism reigns. But paying for the training forces one to care after graduation. Patients were often unwitting victims of these dynamics. The short office visits, the delayed letters and responses. The physician inundated with letters, refills, pressured to fit more patients into the day or penalized for poorer production. Disciplined for underbilling and not having high enough patient experience ratings. The bars become more and more unobtainable. Insurance companies calling the shots, with higher out of pocket expenditures. The distance between physician and patient increasing to great chasms. There still were a few who resisted the system to hold onto the relationships, the relieving of pain and disease, understanding the privilege of being part of the patient's journey. Sharing your journey and the wisdom gained along the way. Dr Meyer was this kind of doctor. Emily hoped that she could be half as good one day. The attending, Doctor Jessup, was not this kind of physician. Emily made her way to the front desk in the lobby, badge in hand.

"Hello, I am scheduled to work with Doctor Jessup today." Dr Jessup mostly spent his time at a comfortable private clinic but one day a week he needed to cover the county clinic. He carried out this task in order to fulfil his teaching requirements so he could one day move to an administrative position, away from the messiness and risk of clinical work. The woman at the desk looked as worn as her surroundings.

"Come back through here," she said as she motioned for Emily to make her way through the door into the clinic. "His desk is down the main hallway on the left."

Dr Jessup was already at his desk. He looked up when Emily made her way down the hallway. "Get a chair." She grabbed one of the metal chairs and sat down. "I expect my residents to be on time, more than on time."

"I'm sorry, this is my first day back after a family crisis and I..."

"You need to learn that medicine comes first. If you want to survive, that is," he said before she could offer a full explanation.

"Yes."

"Dr Meyer said good things about you, but you're not off to a very impressive start." Before she could respond, he handed her a patient chart. She reviewed the presenting complaint and then her past medical history, medications, problems list and allergies. It takes looking at several notes and types of visits to get a good idea of who the patient was. "Come on, we don't have all day. You need to see the patient and get on to the next one."

On that note, Emily went in to see her first patient, Iris, a fifty-three-year-old woman with increasing headaches and intermittent blurry vision, with scalp tenderness. She was reported to live in a nearby shelter, it was unclear why she was living in the shelter. Mental illness, drug addiction, poor health and no safety net, the list was endless. Often you would never know. They brought patients to the clinic twice a week for basic health care.

"Hello Iris, how are you? I see that you have been having headaches, can you tell me about them?" Iris wore a bright green knitted hat and a misbuttoned floral shirt with a faded brown corduroy skirt. She looked significantly older than her fifty-three years. She bore the signs of tragedy. Of hardship. Her slowness in gait reflected the weariness which clung to her as powerfully as the smell of urine.

Iris smiled with a jack-o'-lantern, gappy smile. "Hi doctor, I have godawful headaches. They've been happening for a while."

"What do you mean by a while? A week, a month or a year?"

Iris shrugged her shoulders. "I dunno, a month I think."

"Okay, how often are you having headaches?"

"I dunno, it just hurts."

"I know, Iris, I just want to help, so you aren't having so much pain. The more information you can give me, the more I can try to figure this out and help your pain. Where on your head do you get the headaches?"

"I dunno," said Iris, her crystal blue eyes filling with tears. "It just hurts."

"I'm sorry, Iris, I know you are hurting, and I know you are doing your best. I appreciate that you are working so hard to be helpful. Now take a big breath and let it out slowly." Iris inhaled loudly and exhaled with a sputter. "Can you show me where it hurts? Did you fall and hurt your head? Are you having any weakness? Or problems seeing? Any vomiting, especially in the morning?"

Iris pointed to the left side of her head. "I had a daughter who would be 'bout your age. She died when she was only seven years old. She got that pulmonia. She was real pretty and had long gold hair. She would cry if I tried to cut it, so I just let it grow. She loved peanut butter toast." Emily tried to redirect Iris back to her medical history, but Iris was lost in the vivid reminiscence of her daughter. Iris could almost feel the silkiness of her daughter's gilded hair between her fingers and could smell the honeysuckle scent. Emily watched helplessly while Iris was nodding and smiling to her own inner dialogue. Emily hoped it was good. Iris looked as though she could use something good to ponder.

"Iris, you need to help me figure out your pain."

"I don't think anyone will ever figure that one out," was all Iris said, her eyes once again glistening with moisture. Emily turned her attention to carrying out a neurological examination, it was grossly normal except for pain when she pressed on her left temporal area. Emily could not tell if this was from pain or she just didn't want her to press on her head. Emily could not get an adequate examination of her vision either. When Emily was finished, she found Dr Jessup who was entertaining a couple of sycophantic residents.

"Dr Jessup, I have seen the fifty-three-year-old woman with headaches. The one from the shelter."

"Oh, good. So, don't just stand there, tell me about the patient."

"She is a fifty-three-year-old woman with worsening headaches and visual changes of uncertain duration, I was only able to obtain a limited history from Iris and a carer from the shelter. The headaches can occur at any time of the day, they are so intense that she is woken from sleep, they seem to be temporal — but this is only a guess from how she was holding her head while she was crying and pulled away during the exam. She has stopped combing her hair from the discomfort as per the staff member front the shelter. She does not seem to be able to describe aggravating or alleviating factors. She has a history of..."

"Emily, so what do think she has?"

"There are several possible diagnoses including effects of untreated hypertension, migraines, cluster headaches, temporal arteritis, a space occupying lesion, infection, trauma. I would like imaging, labs, and a surgical consult for a temporal artery biopsy, if her labs suggest inflammation. I believe this is important as she is a relatively poor historian and she may not follow up for further care if she is not evaluated today. Also, she is complaining about changes in her vision in conjunction with her headaches which clearly indicates...".

"Emily, does she have insurance?" , Dr Jessop interrupting impatiently.

"I don't know, but she would most likely qualify for..."

"Emily, her headaches are most likely related to lifestyle factors, she lives in a shelter, you said. What do you think about her nutrition, drugs or alcohol, and mental health? You said she was crying when explaining her symptoms, labile moods and confusion are par for the course with these shelter patients. Call social work and psychiatry."

"Dr Jessup, I am concerned that she came into clinic with these headaches as she doesn't usually come into clinic, so I am worried that they are severe and worsening. Don't you think we should investigate further?"

Dr Jessup looking over at the other two residents said, "You can tell she hasn't been working out in the community long. What patients would you like to present, to demonstrate to the newbie how it's done in this clinic?" They each spewed out a predictable history and examination of a patient with hypertension on a beta blocker and a statin and a patient seen for sinus infection and a UTI. Emily could feel her cheeks burn. She thanked Dr Jessup for the advice and instruction. Emily was aware that medicine was a lot like the military. Everyone needed to respect their position. A clear hierarchy needed to be maintained for patient safety and to provide scaffolding for training. However, one moved through the ranks fairly quickly in medicine. The 'see one, do one, teach one' principle. It seemed way too sudden that you were responsible for fragile human lives. There would be days and sometimes weeks of routine conditions with a straightforward treatment and expected recovery. These times were usually punctuated with the rare and sick patients where you use every bit of the knowledge of basic sciences and medical knowledge gleaned from medical school and experience on the floor to make the diagnosis and treat disease. To hold it at bay for a little longer. To be triumphant over death, one more time. To take away suffering. This is what makes all of it worthwhile. This is more valuable than the money or status. It is that crossroads of pain versus comfort. Of disease versus health. Of life versus death. Most are in awe of the sheer magnitude of these battles. It is easier to focus on the lab work or the imaging, 'the job', and to ignore the frail mortality that we will all eventually face. Most doctors have faith of some kind during these moments. Even if they only have faith in the science. Emily would sometimes pray, but the prayers were generally a list of requests and a vague optimism that someone or something might hear them. The prayers were scattered into the air without much hope of a return. Some days there would be a moment of real hope and maybe a feeling of familiarity, but these times were fleeting and far between. Maybe this lack of belief fed the mental fatigue and sadness. A time when you feel so small and impotent, when the need you see is so great. No matter how hard you work, how many books and articles you read, missed family functions, damaged personal relationships, it will not ever be enough. What you can do is do what you know is the best course of action and hope that it will be good enough. Emily could feel the gentle, oppressive grey fog descend upon her, causing her heart to ache and her shoulders to slump under the weight.

"Dr Jessup, I think she needs a further work up," said Emily quietly at first. "We *need* to evaluate this patient", she said more forcefully.

"What do you want to do, princess?"

"I would like to carry out some simple labs, ESR, CBC, basic metabolic panel, urine analysis, surgical consult, and head imaging."

"Oh, is that all," he smirked to his audience.

"I would hate see something happen to this patient and not be able to give a credible account to a tribunal or M and M meeting." A morbidity and mortality meeting is for clinicians (and administration) and is designed to ascertain cause of an iatrogenic illness or death.

Dr Jessup's eyes flashed in recognition of the thinly veiled threat. "Okay, Dr Warrington, you may proceed, but I will see you at rounds this evening back at the hospital."

"But this is a clinic rotation."

"Someone who is clearly so dedicated to patient care shouldn't mind."

"I have to pick up my children by six p.m."

"Oh, I guess you are going to have to call and make other arrangements. Unless you don't really want to be a doctor."

Emily knew this was the price for Iris's tests. She was just hoping that the open hostility would not last the entire month. He had to re-assert his dominance with respect to their relative positions. She had made him look weaker and for this she would pay. Emily dialed Mrs Lundgren's number and hoped she would allow the kids to stay until she was able to pick them up. Emily's abdomen was tightening with the thought that she just might say 'no'. Emily heard the phone ring and a clipped, "Hello, Lundgren residence".

"Mrs Lundgren, I will be home late could Oliver and Rachel stay with you until seven or eight?"

"I have plans at eight p.m. so you would need to be here by seven thirty."

"Thanks, Mrs Lundgren, I will be there." Emily called Amy and asked if she could pick the children up if she could not get there in time. She readily agreed. At least that much was sorted out. The rest of the day progressed predictably, Emily presented a patient and Dr Jessup picked apart her presentation and plan for each patient. Great first day back. Emily called the shelter and consulted the hospitalist on duty at the hospital for Iris to be admitted for further testing and a possible biopsy of her temporal artery. Untreated Iris could lose her vision or even have a stroke. She would need to be started on high dose steroids and IV fluids if positive. Emily mentioned the plan to Dr Jessup who said he would handle 'it' and discuss the situation with the attending. Emily did not care about being pushed out, she only wanted Iris to be evaluated and treated. She just hoped that Dr Jessup would pass on the correct information.

She made her way to the hospital and arrived on the fourth floor, where the medicine patients were admitted. Emily went through the patient lists and saw only three patients from their group. They had already been seen and had routine conditions such as pneumonia, ileus on bowel rest and intermittent suction, and an asthmatic who was currently stable. She walked to the desk where the hospitalist was sitting. Emily went through the patients and nothing more was to be done this evening. "Hi, I'm Emily Warrington, I am the senior resident working with Dr Jessup." She extended her hand to the weary attending with a five o'clock shadow and a Styrofoam cup half-filled with dark syrupy coffee. He didn't look up.

"Dr Jessup isn't on service this week," he said flatly.

"He told me to meet him here to go over the patients on the floor," Emily explained.

"What did you do to annoy him?"

"What do you mean?"

"He always jerks around the residents who have offended him in some way. What did you do?"

"I made him evaluate a patient."

"Oh, that would do it. He's a jackass. Just don't provoke him too much. He can be pretty vindictive."

"Thanks for the advice." Emily grabbed her coat and her bag and made her way out of the hospital. Traffic was heavy and Emily could feel her stress level climbing with each tedious mile. All she could think about was getting to Oliver and Rachel. She had gone to work most every day since they were born. It was more her typical routine. She had never felt more unsettled. The unease would not go away. The last time she had gone to work she came home to the police in her driveway. Her heart started to beat harder and faster. Emily could feel her stomach contents rising into her throat. She was able to swallow air and force the bile down. Emily thought about coming home to Luke and the kids. When Luke was Luke. When he still loved her. When they were a family. Emily's anger towards Luke was lessening. Sheer grief was taking over. For today anyway. She wanted to talk to him about her day, and what a jerk Jessup was. And make dinner together. To feel the warmth of their familiarity. To have someone to help bear the trials of this life. Luke. His smile. His shared memories of their children, of their youth, of their common journey. Emily felt the hot tears make their way down her cheeks. Her throat constricting. How could Luke leave? How could he put them in this situation? How could God let this happen? Was He even there? Less than a month ago she had a husband, a secure and defined future, financial stability, an intact family. Now, she could not even be sure how she was going provide for her children. She didn't know what she could trust. What was real. She was all her children had and she felt deep despair for this realty. She was just holding it together. She could feel herself hyperventilate and the pain in her chest from a renewed revelation of their loss and how their lives would never again be the same. She pulled over as her vision was clouded by the tears. She no longer fought them and they fell unchecked. She sobbed large gasping sobs. The kind she would never allow herself at home. In case someone would hear her desperation.

"Damn him!" she said with her anger returning. Emily saw the time on the dashboard. She needed to get Oliver and Rachel. She took some deep breaths and wiped her face. She texted Amy to pick up the children. It was almost eight p.m. Emily hoped that Amy would pick them up as soon as possible. She could not afford to offend Mrs Lundgren. Time was running out to find another babysitter for her children. This was more difficult in view of her limited funds. Her head hurt from the tears and the intense contemplation. Amy's text that she had picked up the children lit up her screen. Emily was so relieved she could've kissed Amy. She pulled up to Amy's little house. She was looking forward to holding Oliver and Rachel and make the long day melt away into the three of them. They were what was best in her life. Her ache for being with them had increased over the past few weeks. She ran up to the door and knocked hurriedly. Amy answered the door and Emily could just see Oliver watching TV in the living room. The disorganization caught Emily off guard as she had forgotten how messy Amy was in her personal life. She was fastidious in her work, but home was another matter. She could see Rachel sleeping on the couch with a blanket and a McDonald's cheeseburger wrapper. At least they had dinner.

Oliver ran over to Emily and hugged her. "Mommy! I missed you."

"I missed you too, baby."

"Emily, could I talk to you?" asked Amy in hushed tones pointing towards the kitchen.

"Sure."

"Emily, I don't think it is good for the kids to be at Mrs Lundgren's house with Abby there. I think she is up to something," said Amy, elaborating further in hushed tones. "I went to pick up the kids and Mrs Lundgren was arguing with Abby, I could hear them shouting but couldn't quite make out what they were saying. I could just decipher that it was about some money and that Abby refused to pay it back. Mrs Lundgren was shouting, and Abby slammed the door and drove off in a panic. Oliver and Rachel were crying. I grabbed their stuff and brought them here. Rachel had a soaking wet diaper and a raw diaper rash. I put her in the bath and put on some ParaGard cream. They were both really hungry, so they had McDonald's. I hope that is okay. I had some ramen noodles but they both looked unimpressed."

"Thanks Amy, that's fine. I am glad you were there." Emily was trying to get her head around the day's events and that her children had been left to fend for themselves. Emily felt a pang of guilt. She had persuaded Mrs Lundgren to watch Oliver and Rachel. Amy could see the panic on Emily's face.

"Hey, I could watch them tomorrow. Tuesday is my new day off."

"Thanks, Amy."

"Emily, I don't trust Abby. I don't know if I should say anything as it could have been innocent."

"Well..." Emily said expectantly. "Come on Amy, you can't finish a sentence like that without filling in the details."

"It's just that Abby and Luke seemed cozy when I had come over to talk to you about my joyful divorce. They seemed flustered or disheveled when they came to the door. I could have misread the situation, but I just don't trust her." Amy looked away.

"Why didn't you say anything before?"

"I didn't want to cause drama without proof, I was also afraid I was reading too much into it considering my wreck of a marriage."

"You could have told me that you had seen Abby at my house and that she seemed 'cozy' with Luke." Emily immediately regretted the tone she had taken with Amy. Her only real friend at the moment. She had protected Oliver and Rachel. "I'm sorry Amy. It is just that everything is so chaotic and so hard. I think I am losing my mind some days. I don't know what is real any more."

"I know. It's okay." Emily could hear Rachel stirring and calling for Emily. She collected their things and gathered them into the car.

They were all quiet on the ride home. Emily wasn't sure if she should bring up the events at Mrs Lundgren's or let it lie. She decided to let it lie for the moment, she was far too exhausted to go through all of the details and more importantly she did not want to upset them further. She parked up as close as she could to the front step. Emily picked Rachel up and walked behind Oliver who was running towards the door. The door was partially open. Emily felt cold when she walked through the door. She held Oliver's hand tightly and pushed him behind her while she carried Rachel close to her. It was dark but she could make out pieces of the lamp on the floor by the table in the entry way and could hear footsteps. "Oliver stay behind me. "Shhhh." She motioned to Oliver. "Is anyone here? Who is there? Who is there? Get out of my house!" she shouted.

Emily could see a shadowy figure and then heard a crash and the back door slamming and then reopening. She looked out the window with her heart still racing. She saw a dark-haired man maybe six feet tall running into a vehicle and then screeching off. He looked at Emily before getting into the car, he looked familiar although she couldn't quite make out his features in the dark. His dark eyes chilled her to the bone. He was gone before she could shout at him further. She could just make out a black Nissan, possibly an Altima or Maxima, it was difficult to tell. Emily could just make out the first three letters of the license plate: LGH. The plate was from one of the Carolinas, she couldn't make out the rest. Emily turned on the lights. In the living room the couches had been overturned and the coffee table broken into two pieces. The framed photograph of Rachel and Oliver at the beach had the glass shattered and the frame smashed on the floor where someone had stepped on it. Emily moved through the carnage into the kitchen where there were broken glasses and the toaster on the floor. The door was wide open. Emily closed the door. She looked around at their house, their home. Their cherished memories smashed.

Oliver looked up at Emily. "Mommy, what happened? Why did that man break our stuff? He's in big trouble," Oliver said as he was shaking his head. "Mommy is he coming back?" Rachel started to cry.

Emily grabbed Oliver and Rachel and hastily threw a few items of clothing and toys into the car and started to drive. She called nine-one-one and gave them as many details as she could recall. She drove to the closest police station to complete the report. The station was filled with men and women in uniform who effused detached efficiency. Emily and the children were brought to the desk of a balding and tired looking detective.

"Okay, ma'am. What do you know about the perpetrator with the black Nissan?"

"What? I don't know anything about him except he was in my house." Emily went through the sequence of her day which resulted in the coming home to the said individual being in her house and her calling the police and then leaving with her children. He looked quizzical but did not comment further. Once Emily had completed the questioning, she left the police station. After they were secured in the car, Emily started to drive off but didn't know where she was going. She had seen a Country Suites not far from the police station. Its appeal being its proximity. She parked in the semi-lit parking lot and signed in at the front desk. With the key card in her hand, she unloaded the children and scarce supplies into the standard, beige room. Once she had the kids settled and they were sleeping, the events of the day churned around in her brain over and over again. She showered and made some tea, but sleep escaped her burdened mind. She looked at the clock, it was two a.m. and then three a.m. She managed to drift off to a restless sleep at some point during the night.

The alarm clock sounded off with a loud beep. She needed to remind herself of the happenings of the day before and their current location. She panicked and then saw Oliver and Rachel entangled in the blankets and she relaxed slightly. Her babies were with her. They were together. She went over to the coffee maker and put the coffee bag in the basket and poured some cloudy water into the container.

She looked for their toothbrushes and clothes. Rachel only had one sock and Oliver's were odd. The clothes did not match but at least they were warm. There had been a recent cold snap. Typical for early springtime in Minnesota. Winter would keep its hold as long as it could. Eventually it would give way to summer, with only a sliver of spring and a fierce seasonal battle in between. Emily was relying on this randomness as a source of comfort. Tomorrow it could be almost summer. She listened for the sputtering of water to signify that the coffee was made. She drank the weak coffee and called Oliver to get up. She handed him his clothing. Emily would dress Rachel, who was reluctant to get up and start moving. She hurried out of the hotel for check out. She would take the children over to Amy's and figure out tomorrow later today.

She pulled up to Amy's and knocked on the door. After several minutes, Amy appeared looking more disheveled than usual. "Hi Emily, to what do I owe this pleasure at this time of the morning?"

"Hi Amy. You do remember that you said you would watch the kids today, right?"

"No, but okay. Hi kids," she said waving at Oliver and Rachel. Emily brought the kids into the house and tried to avert her eyes from last night's dishes on the coffee table and general disarray.

"Thanks Amy." Emily got back in the car and drove to the clinic for round two with Dr Jessup. She was hoping for a better time today. She would need to keep her mouth shut and be deferential, even if it killed her.

She was five minutes late by the time she got to the clinic and parked. "Ugh." She murmured as she made her way into the clinic. Jessup's group of minions were already surrounding him. She could feel their derisive stares as she made her way down the corridor. Another day. "Oh, Doctor Warrington, how good of you to join us. I thought I made it clear yesterday that you that rounds start at seven thirty, not seven thirty-two and certainly not seven thirty-five."

"Yes, Dr Jessup I know. I am sorry." He had already moved on by the time she had apologized. He handed Emily her patient list, several patients who were complex and 'difficult'. Emily did not mind this though. She liked the patients that no one wanted. The complicated and hardened patients. Their stories were usually more interesting. They needed more kindness and patience. Unfortunately, they also needed more time, which she did not have. He was setting her up to fail. She would have to keep her head down and do her job without engaging him further. She only needed a further two weeks with him before moving on to the hospital for her final rotation. The morning went quickly with patients, tests, going through prescriptions and results. Dr Jessup mostly ignored her and waved her off when she tried to present her patients. She went ahead with what she thought was the most reasonable plan. She was getting into her own rhythm when he told her to come with him to the hospital to present a patient at the lunchtime meeting. She finished up with her last patient and gathered her bag and coat.

"What patient would you like me to present?"

"You're so brilliant, why don't you surprise me."

"I don't have any X-rays or records or time to prepare a PowerPoint presentation."

He looked at Emily with a tight smile. "Well this is when experience comes in, I guess. It will separate the sheep from the goats, so to speak." Dr Jessup would usually have his residents present for him as he was not interested enough to complete this work himself. He would rarely offer any support in preparation or execution. He seemed to enjoy the failures more than the successes. His fleshy and plethoric face seemed to have a limited number of responses. They generally consisted of smirking, disdain, or condescension and often a combination of all three.

Emily's mind was racing, trying to think of any interesting patients and trying to get their information in time for the meeting. With electronic health records, at least that should be easier. She decided to present Iris and focus on the difficulties of evaluating the homeless patient and providing adequate care to meet their needs. The history, past medical history, medications, vital signs, examination, labs/tests, assessment and plan and follow up were fresh in her memory. She would look up her progress and the results of her testing. Emily would have usually had all of the information locked in her head first thing in the morning, but nothing seemed right or usual. She did not have time to review this information before rounds. She was hoping that she would not be the first presenter. Emily was not a natural public speaker. She was reminded of this early in her residency. Over time, she had become a welcome and highly rated speaker due to her story-telling approach. It was the only way that she managed her anxiety. She simply told the story of her patient. The story included the clinical aspects of how they presented with the biochemical, pathological, pharmacological, genetic, sociological and psychological aspects of the illness. She emphasized each facet as relevant to the specific patient. She also included barriers to optimal treatment as it is integral to their overall story. You could be a brilliant diagnostician but if your patient could not afford their medication, it would not change their outcome. It may not change the outcome in any case as there are often so many variables. Where they live. Do they have reliable housing, food sources, transportation? Do they have constant stress? Do they even believe in the treatment? How can you prescribe out of poverty and so many other obstacles? Emily felt weary thinking about these facts. She would focus on what she could do. On providing the best chance possible.

Her mind was drawn back to the present and her imminent presentation. She finally found Iris's chart in the system. She had received one dose of steroids and was discharged by Dr Abbott, no surgical consult. Emily could not believe her eyes. How could someone have discharged her before evaluating her or treating her? Emily looked at her CRP which was twenty times the normal limit and her ESR was highly elevated at 110 mm/h-. They had just become available with her refresh icon; they had been ordered as routine rather than stat. She had been discharged before these results were known. Emily saw that Iris was in the emergency department currently with acute onset vision loss and right-sided facial drop and weakness. Emily felt sick and could feel an anger rise up in her like vitriol.

She stormed into the conference room and asked to speak to Dr Abbott. A second-year resident who was sat in the Jessop corner of the conference room. "How could you discharge a patient without knowing her results with those symptoms? Her ESR and CRP were significantly elevated in addition to her headaches and blurry vision"

"Oh, Emily what are you talking about," said Dr Jessup interrupting her invective. Dr Jessop looked around the room at the other physicians who were quieting at the sheer anger in Emily's voice. "This is Emily Warrington, fourth-year resident and seldom on time. Who thinks she knows it all."

"Dr Jessop, that patient you had your resident so carelessly discharge is in the ED with acute onset blindness and right-sided weakness. You knew that she most likely had temporal arteritis, because I told you that, but you didn't care. Now she is homeless and blind and maybe having a stroke. She came to us for help and you failed to give her the most basic standard of care."

"Emily your position as a resident on my service is terminated. I suggest you leave immediately."

Emily knew she had gone too far but couldn't stop herself from responding. "Dr Jessup you are a reckless, greedy, and incompetent man who should not be allowed anywhere near patients. I may have to leave but at least I haven't blinded someone!" Emily grabbed her coat and bag and stormed out of the conference room. On her way to her car her anger was dissipating and was replaced with the shock of what she had just done. She would have to call Ashley and beg for another rotation, if that were even possible. In a little over one month, Emily's carefully planned life had unraveled to threads. Threads that were frayed and disconnected. A career that was almost coming to fruition. Safety. It was an illusion, but she had trusted in that illusion. Her home had been intact, her life on track.

Emily called Ashley in the hope of reaching her before Jessop did. The inevitable dread manifesting as a lump in her throat. Emily made her way to her car and got into the front seat and took a few deep breaths and tentatively dialed Ashley's number. It had transferred to voice mail with Ashley's sugary message. "Hello Ashley, this is Emily..."

Ashley answered before Emily could complete the sentence. "Hello, Emily, you seemed to have got yourself in quite the pickle." Emily's annoyance at the term 'pickle' was suppressed to allow Ashley to finish her lecture on good resident behavior. "Emily, Dr Jessop is a respected attending and he was very upset with your behavior. He said you 'lost it' in front of a room full of attendings. He suggested that you have a mental health evaluation before returning to the program. He, however, doesn't think you are fit to continue the program."

Emily could feel her heart beating faster. Her hands were clenched. "Ashley, I am sorry that I went off like that. You know things have been hard lately with my husband *dying and all.*"

"Emily, I think you have worn out all of our good will in the department."

"Ashley, couldn't you discuss this with Dr Meyer or Dr Fishman? They both know that I am a good resident."

"I'm afraid I can't Emily. I have been offered the attending position with Dr Meyer as your emotional state has been so uncertain over this past month. I thought I would help and relieve some of the pressure and talked to Dr Meyer myself. He was more than happy to offer me the position. So, you see, I wouldn't want to jeopardize my own future as well."

"You conniving snake! You wanted that position for yourself this whole time. That is why you have been so unhelpful. How do you sleep at night?"

"Toodles." And then Ashley had cut the call off. Emily redialed several times but was met with a, *'This number is unauthorized to complete this call'* message. How could this be happening? She felt panic but then it quickly subsided. Emily was getting used to the feelings of shock and panic.

Chapter 15
End of the Beginning

The gravity of the situation had not fully penetrated her brain. She shrugged off the weight of the circumstances and put the key into the ignition and drove home. It was not home, it was the facade in which they played their parts in their own reality show. The deception of normality. Now it was a source of pain and a reminder of betrayal and fear. The already strained house was now in a state of complete disorder. Emily would not take Oliver and Rachel to stay in that shell again. She would go there now and get what they needed. She would get her severance pay and they would leave. She walked into the house, a routine occurrence carried out hundreds of times before. Now she was aware of every movement and fiber of matter. The wall color and the small scratches on the wall where Oliver had hit the area with his cars. The stains on the carpet that Emily had tried to remove, leaving the faint orange of spaghetti sauce. The nicks on the cupboards. The numerous small defects that had together told the story of the family that had lived in this house. Emily came to get what they would need. She grabbed three suitcases and randomly filled them with clothing and stuffed toys and books. She went into Luke's office and grabbed his computer from his bottom drawer. As she pulled the computer out from under an array of papers in the top drawer, the bottom of the drawer had become dislodged. Emily pulled hard and the bottom had pulled away from the frame. Underneath the false bottom, there were several letters. They were in Luke's handwriting and addressed to Emily, a couple to his mother, and to Oliver and Rachel. Emily grabbed them and shoved them into a bag. Under the letters, she could just make out an official looking green paper. Money. Hundred-dollar bills. There were scads of hundred-dollar bills. Emily grabbed a wad of the cash and stuffed the bills into her purse. She would count the money later. She rifled through the other drawers. There was mostly office material and ledgers from his old company and a couple of keys, which looked like they were from lockers. A few brown packages were under the cash, but Emily just left these where she found them. A Christmas card dropped onto the floor from a stack of papers on the glass top of the desk. It was from her mother. She looked at the card and saw the address on the envelope. Emily grabbed the envelope and shoved it in with the other papers and keys. She picked up the suitcases and hastily threw them into the trunk of her car. She looked back at the house as she pulled away. She didn't feel nostalgic, she felt relief to be getting away from the nightmare of the past weeks. Once again, their lives would never be the same.

She went into the bank and deposited enough cash to pay the bills for the next few weeks. She also went to a cleaning company to remove the chaos from the house, after the police were finished, so the house could be sold. She had several thousand left after these expenditures. She tucked the cash into a plain white envelope which she carefully placed in zipped compartment of her purse.

Emily picked up Oliver and Rachel from Amy's house. They were both playing on the floor with the cat trying to teach her how to do tricks. Amy looked at Emily and shrugged her shoulders. The cat seemed more than a little miffed at the unsolicited attention. Emily did not want to go into the details of the day's events as it happened so fast and Emily hadn't processed the consequences fully herself. She was also hoping to avoid further judgement.

"Hi Amy. I hope they were well-behaved today?"

"Oh, yeah. They have been watching TV for hours." Emily looked away so Amy could not see the disapproval flash in her eyes. "You are back earlier than I expected. What, did Jessop cut you some slack?"

"Something like that. Come on Rachel and Oliver lets go."

"Did you figure out what you're going to do about the break in? You can't stay there."

"I know Amy, we are on our way to a hotel until the place is safe. Thanks again for watching the kids." Amy looked quizzically at Emily.

"I know you're not telling me everything, but I am going to assume you have your reasons." Amy looked into Emily's eyes as if trying to see the truth in the pigment. Emily hugged Amy and thanked her again. Oliver was already running out to the car and Emily picked up Rachel and made her way out the door. Emily looked at the postmark of her mother's address: 1854 Heron Drive, Ashton Island, SC. Emily had no idea what this town would be like. She had never been to the South except Florida which did not really count. This is due to the large number of refugees from the cold North living there, making the culture more of a warm North mix, socially speaking. She felt a catch of anxiety but then it was gone. She did not have the luxury of fear. She had her life collapse around her and all that was holding her together was her responsibility for Oliver and Rachel. They deserved a functional parent. To be shielded from the betrayals and sorrows of life. At least from further pain and disappointment. If they were together, they would be okay. It was liberating in some ways. She did not have to think about finding childcare. No incompetent and disparaging attendings. Just them. Emily could not think about what she was going to do for a job or her residency. Her student loans. Right now, she just wanted to get away with her babies. To get away from the ache that had become her new normal. The reminders of all of her failures. As a physician Emily had become used to holding back. When reviewing an abnormal blood test, you go through all of the possibilities and try to exclude the most dangerous first. You do not tell the patient that you think they may have cancer, but you tell them that you need to do further tests to help understand what is causing their problem. Why cause so much pain over an unlikely event. You also get a chance to slowly ease them into the possibility of a more serious illness. Later you offer this as part of the differential diagnosis should this become more likely, delicately and stealthily broaching their worst fears. You get to test the waters to see what they know and what they want to know. You ask questions and move forward deliberately. You balance between truth and compassion. You hold back. This is one of the greatest skills learned in medical practice. In life. How to hold back.

She glanced back at Oliver and Rachel. Oliver's fair hair, impossibly straight and partially covering his eyes. Rachel and her chocolate brown loose curls and large brown eyes. Oliver looked so much like Luke it was startling at times. It brought back the familiar hurt in her heart. The longing for Luke and then the pain of betrayal. A reminder of their fragile lives. Like a well-placed house of cards with the appearance of being solid until a breeze comes and dismantles everything in one foul swoop. The destruction so complete it leaves no evidence that there was ever a structure there in the first place. This is our lives now Emily thought. She drove instinctively, periodically looking back at Oliver and Rachel.

Chapter 16
The Journey to the South

Only an hour in to the journey Oliver started complaining that he needed to pee. Rachel agreed that he should pee. Oliver said he was hungry as well. She was not sure if he really needed to meet either of the physical demands, or just wanted a break from the car. Emily looked for a place to stop. They approached a low budget chain restaurant and she brought both children into the shabby woman's bathroom. Emily felt it better to contend with disapproving stares rather than not being with her child. The food was tasteless and soggy, but the wait staff were pleasant and efficient. Emily paid the tab and fastened both children into their respective car seats. Emily swiped for Siri to restart the journey to South Carolina. She would try to clear Wisconsin and stay in Illinois overnight. This was now her new quest. If she could think in terms of shorter goals, it helped to soften the dread. Dread over what she was going to do for employment and how she was going to take care of Oliver and Rachel. Her babies. She was alone with her children. She didn't have a phone number for her mother, and she couldn't find her number with various search engines. All she had was an address. She hoped she would still be there; she had not worked it through what they would do if she had moved on. The last letter Emily had read made it appear that her mother was living by herself in her own home. Hopefully, reality will agree with the impression. It had been before the kids were born that she had last seen her mother. Her mother had been with some guy who was living off her and an alcoholic so pretty much her mother's usual type. Her mother's desperation had been palpable. Her mother, Beatrice or Bea, was sociable between relationships. She rapidly created connections. Superficial temporary connections. She had an easy smile and an infectious laugh. She was always looking to form support networks, rapidly and widely. Like a ball being supported by colorful wooden sticks, as soon as one is removed, another is added to bear the weight. The weight is lessened by the number of sticks, but fluid, one leaves, and another takes the position. This alters the location but only gradually. The loss of one support is bearable, you just keep changing the sticks. All the supports being equally interchangeable. The one exception was with Emily. Beatrice had loved Emily. She just could not take care of her. She could not take care of herself. But she loved her daughter. Her one accomplishment in life for which she was proud.

Emily felt tired. The kids were quiet for the moment. They have been through so much. The signs for the Wisconsin Dells caught her eye. This was a place she had associated with happiness and comfort. She turned off the highway. This is where they would stay tonight. She made her way to Baraboo and found the Kalahari resort.

It looked imposing and garish with multiple African themed buildings extending to a movie theatre. Emily parked up and booked one of the more expensive suites. She bought all of them new bathing suits, all cash from the brightly colored gift shop.

"Is this where we are going to live?" asked Oliver hopefully.

"No sweetie, but we are going to live here for tonight." She found the room. It had African inspired decor consistent with the resort theme. There were two queen-sized beds and a couch with a coffee table a large flat screen TV and a kitchenette with coffee and tea. Oliver and Rachel ran into the room and proceeded to jump on the bed. Emily put on their new swimsuits and they went down to the waterpark. She brought them over to the children's wading area where there were several children splashing in the warm water. Emily held Rachel's hand until she squirmed free.

"Thank you, Mommy," Rachel said not looking up but smiling at the colorful molded frogs in the water.

"It's okay baby." Emily sat in the shallow water watching the children play. It was the first time in a month that she felt a hint of the stress easing. The loud sounds of children laughing and rushing water prevented deep thought. The brightly colored slides and walls made it feel like a vacation at the seaside. A tacky and joyful retreat. After she held them in the floating figure-eight on the lazy river they seemed to be tiring. Emily scooped up Rachel and grabbed Oliver's hand and walked them back to the room. She bathed them and showered herself. It was still only around nine p.m. They would normally be in bed asleep, but Emily did not want to waste this time. She then remembered that they were on their own time, for the moment at least. She had only brought a couple of books. Their favorite books that she had read to them so many times that the pages were torn, and the scented areas had lost their fragrance long ago. They seemed satisfied. She would order room service for a late snack or dinner. They hadn't eaten much at the restaurant on the way. She ordered typical kid fare. Macaroni and cheese for Rachel and a ham and cheese sandwich for Oliver. She had grabbed an activity guide for the kids. Easter egg dyeing and several other crafty events were available. Emily had nearly forgotten that it would be Easter in a couple of days. Time had gone so fast and so drawn out at the same. Time did not have any real meaning. It certainly did not seem the comforting linear process that Emily had come to expect. It seemed eons ago that she was a blissfully unaware mother of two, a wife. That the plans of being an attending and providing for her family comfortably were faded pipe dreams. Unreal. The thoughts of where she was would catch her out and felt like a punch in the gut. She would push it out of her mind once again to avoid the terror that was barely contained. Right now, she would watch *Despicable Me 2* with her babies. Watching their faces, engrossed in the melodic exaggerated accents and the simple improbable story line. They seemed unaware of the turmoil in their lives for the time being. They would stay another night so they could dye Easter eggs. Right now, they were homeless.

They were not afforded the simple luxuries of dyeing Easter eggs, of going grocery shopping, of hanging their backpacks on hooks in the hallway and so many other routines that require a home. Emily had to physically shake her head and rub her eyes to stop that thought process or the grief would become unbearable. Her fear and loneliness would be all consuming. No, she would focus on their beautiful soft faces and hopeful eyes. For right now they were all safe and had each other. She would squeeze out as much happiness as she could in this mess. The eye of the storm, so to speak. Their small fragile family.

    The time evaporated quickly. The egg dyeing and swimming. The ice cream and pizza all blended together into a medley of excess. Emily felt the stay was an almost anointed experience. She had not thought about that term in years. It felt peaceful and right. She even said a prayer for their safe journey to the South. It was a very rudimentary prayer but the first one in a long time. She was energized and Oliver and Rachel were calmer. This was a great combination for the road ahead. The tentative calm did not last long. Rachel did not want Oliver to look at her. Ollie then deliberately would stare at her as close to her face as he could whilst still being in his booster seat. This resulted in many shouts and screams. Emily did stop the vehicle to get out to take a few deep breaths. There were stops for food and toileting, but they were making good progress overall. The scenery changing slowly but undeniably. The dirty snow of Minnesota and Wisconsin were replaced with the bedraggled grass of spring in Illinois giving way to the balmy warmth of the South. I felt balmy to Emily after the frigid north, but the temperatures were in the fifties and sixties. Emily remembered that she had an aunt in Illinois but could not quite remember her name so the thought of visiting her flashed in her mind and then was gone as quickly as it came. The monotonous drive had allowed her brain to reminisce and wander. She was getting used to the gentle background hum of being on the road. Short-term goals of reaching a specific town had become reassuring. For the first time in her life, she was only thinking short-term. Anything beyond this was confusing and anxiety provoking. She did not have their lives mapped out more than the next day. She was thankful for the interruptions of her children on the journey. She had taken her time allowing them to savor their surroundings. To get dirty and to play childish games. Her thoughts were disrupted by the sudden onslaught of hunger pangs. She was reminded that she missed breakfast in the commotion of getting their stuff together to check out of the hotel. She had grabbed a small muffin and fruit cocktail for the children which they instantly devoured. She mostly wanted coffee. She decided to turn off the main highway onto a side street of a small town. The town was nostalgic of small-town America. Old brick buildings and a comfortable pace. The main street which was conveniently called Main Street had a few shops and a Starbucks — no getting away from some things — and a bank. A non-chain cafe was just off of the main drag. The children were impressed by the brightly colored seating and 'fifties' charm and black duct tape over the red vinyl seats. The waitress was capable and patient. Oliver wanted chicken nuggets after changing his mind three or four times and Rachel wanted a chocolate chip pancake. Emily ordered a fluffy omelet breakfast with hash browns and pancakes. The coffee was strong and fresh. The food came out of the kitchen reasonably fast and the homemade syrup was delicious. Emily gave up on the enormous portion halfway through the meal. She had lost fifteen pounds since Luke's death. She thought the wonderful smelling food would be sufficient enticement to stimulate her appetite. She just could not overcome the state of deprivation to which her body had become accustomed. Emily was thankful this problem had not affected Oliver or Rachel. They both ate well with many crumbs falling on their clothes and evidence of their meals over their faces. Emily brought them into the rest room and cleaned them up, paid the tab and then left.

Emily had their short-term target in her mind. They would travel to Kentucky by nightfall. Emily pushed out the dread once again of how crazy this was. Going to her mother's home when she had not spoken to her for years. When all she had was an address. What if she was in another destructive relationship? Someone who was abusive and defeated. Someone consistent with the reasons that she had left in the first place. Someone who she would never allow around her children. Emily could feel herself breathing faster. She had to turn up the radio and sing to the song to shake this out of her head. Right now, they would make it to Kentucky. The drive was relatively quiet and the roads smooth. She could feel her eyes getting tired and bored from watching the repetitive scenery.

"Mommy I don't want to be in the car any more. I want to go home and play with my friends. I want to go home, to 'Minniesota' " Oliver said with great distress.

"I am sorry Ollie. We will have a new home. One where we can go for walks all year round and you can meet your grandmother. We can even get a cat or a dog at some point."

"Could it be an 'olden reliever?" Oliver asked hopefully.

"Sure. As long as we have room." She could feel the change in his countenance with the anticipation of getting a dog, so she did not want to shatter this fragile shift. She decided to come off at the next town to find a park where Oliver and Rachel could run around and play. They were not on anyone else's time clock. Emily had avoided checking her emails or messages as she did not know how she could explain her irresponsible decisions. She just could not face any more judgement or disappointment right now. She already was using all of her strength to bear the weight of this journey. She did not want another straw to test the stability of her back. When turning off her phone she could see a glimpse of a message from Ashley and several from Amy. She could not make out the others and averted her eyes not to pique her interest to review their content. She instead tucked her phone into her pocket and played with the kids, pushing them on the toddler swings. Oliver objected so strongly that she moved him to the 'big kids' swing while he pumped his legs back and forth. Emily held Rachel in her lap facing her. Emily moved her legs from straight to flexed in a rhythmic fashion which felt exhilarating the higher they went. The cool air and motion aided in lifting the oppression of her circumstance. Hugging Rachel close to her, feeling her warm little body. Her explosions of laughter were salve for their battered souls. They ran and went down the slide and chased each other. Emily hid under the slide and played 'monster under the bridge' and would run out and chase them until they both squealed. She bundled them into the car after they were played out and wanting to go back to the car. She had still hoped to reach Kentucky by nightfall. Emily was enjoying the milder temperatures and the more lilting accents. The matter-of-fact sing-song, slightly nasal accent of Minnesota was nowhere to be heard. This was both comforting and unsettling.

The rest of the drive was uneventful. Emily put the radio on to occupy her mind whilst driving. She found a contemporary Christian station which seemed to be the most soothing. She would sing to the songs and mostly make up the words, but she was quick to learn a few of the lyrics. She had not thought about God in a long time, and now she was thinking about Him on a daily basis. The thoughts brought back the hurt and anger she had suppressed, and she changed the radio station. She had been a Christian once. A real change-your-world-kind of Christian. One that had changed her life at the time. She was a teenager and her friend brought her to youth group when she heard the most powerful message of her short life. She felt compelled by the sheer love and compassion of Jesus. She felt His presence in her life and prayers. This was not the kind of relationship like the reluctant Sunday duty kind of relationship, but an all-consuming transformation. She could not get enough of this amazing sweetness. She was made fun of by her friends and acquaintances for the changes she had made and talking about Jesus as if he were her love of her life. She did not care but it was the cruelty some of the 'Christian' teens had demonstrated to the vulnerable, which eventually caused her to turn away. They acted as if being a 'Christian' gave them entitlement to judge and to show callousness to those who were less fortunate or weak or different, rather than mercy and grace. This should have flowed from them like a river. Emily had seen evidence of these behaviors over and over and eventually she gave up on Christianity altogether. She had witnessed sniggering and been the subject of this more than once. She was poor from a single parent family. She would sometimes be pitied and, on other occasions, judged for the lack of morality of her mother for living with men to whom she wasn't married. She guessed they hadn't read about the Samaritan woman and Jesus. She continued to love Jesus but this too, she would allow to fade over time. Right now, she just felt broken. Would she ever be okay again? Really okay? Emily could not answer this question or others like it or enjoy the self-indulgence of reflection. There was this journey to be pushed through and of course, caring for her babies. She noticed the needle slipping into the empty zone and she started to look for a gas station. She pulled up to a gas station selling produce and bric-a-brac. There was a tanned and unshaven man sat outside the store. He was around sixty-five years old but could have been anywhere from fifty to eighty years old. You could tell by his leathery skin and worn clothing that he had seen some rough times. Beside him were two garbage bags filled with his treasures. He had a mixed breed dog, of medium build who sat at his feet. The dog had a pink jeweled collar and appeared to be well cared for with her coat brushed and her nails clipped. She sat quietly as Emily, Oliver and Rachel walked by.

"Hi puppy," said Rachel as she reached out to the dog, before Emily could intercept her hand. The dog licked her hand and wagged her tail. The man extended his hand to Emily. She shook his hand as he introduced himself.

"Hi, ma'am, I am Art, and this is Maggie. She won't bite. She loves kids. I am just taking a rest here. I rest where I want and go when I want to go. Life is *good*." He elongated the vowels. "Retirement is the best job that I ever had, I get to wake up when I want, go to bed when I want on my own time. My journey is my own." He smiled with a gappy, but fairly white smile. Looking more so against the bronze skin. "Don't you sometimes just want to take off? And enjoy your own company? Being by yourself? You are never really alone though."

"Thanks, for the advice," Emily said as she looked into his eyes. They appeared to hold great thoughtfulness and compassion. Emily noticed his dog tags and guessed some sort of PTSD from the military. She had seen it a number of times before in clinic. He thanked Emily and the kids for talking to him and Maggie. Emily noticed his bright pink nail polish carefully applied, contrasting with his weather-beaten skin. Emily just smiled and moved the children forward into the shop. She selected some reasonably healthy snacks and drinks. She paid cash for the treats and her gas. She did have some money in her account after her recent deposit but felt safer paying cash. She scolded herself for being a tad paranoid but felt less anxious paying in real currency. Whatever Luke was involved with certainly had nothing to do with her and her children. The break in was most likely a coincidence. People have break ins all the time without being part of some larger conspiracy or criminal syndicate. Emily bought extra waters for Art and Maggie. Times were tough but not as tough as they were for Art and his dog. She wondered how long he had been living like this and where he slept at night. His journey was written on his soft shabby face and warm, gentle eyes. His eyes looked familiar somehow. Right now, she needed to get her children into the car and onto the next town on her list. The places on her list were getting further apart. Not because of greater distances or more sparsely populated areas, but because she was losing the heart for it. The plan was going by the wayside like most everything else in the shambles she called a life. She was not so dissimilar from Art after all. Emily had always really known how tenuous porticos were. She pretended not to know this truth and many others like it. She wanted to forget the wounds sustained in uncovering these verities. Pain is a harsh but thorough teacher.

Emily was abruptly thrust out of her thoughts with the squeals of laughter from the back seat. Oliver was making farting sounds which made Rachel think he was the funniest person alive. Emily smiled at their new-found camaraderie, however short-lived. The tires on the road had a calming almost mesmerizing hum. Emily had to shake herself awake at times from the monotony of the reverberations. She thought she would give the kids another hour and stop to get out and walk. She had not quite formed a rhythm to their journey. She was still too fragmented to form any reasonable plan. Oliver and Rachel did not seem to mind unless they were tired, bored or hungry. She was amazed at how resilient they seemed to be. She also knew this was deceptive. Children could appear so calm and accepting until they weren't. This often came in the form of a troubled adolescence. Parental flaws are pushed out to the surface for all to see. I wonder what will surface from my beautiful children. For now, it was enough to hear their laughter from farting noises. After an hour they reached a rest stop which was pretty basic with bathrooms only just above outhouse standards and a vending machine full of chips and chocolate. The children ran and played on the green grass. Emily made sure Oliver had gone to the bathroom and she changed Rachel's diaper. Emily encouraged Rachel to try and sit on the 'potty like a big girl'. Emily tried to appeal to her sense of sibling rivalry by commenting on how Oliver always goes on the potty like a big boy. Rachel seemed unimpressed.

"Would you like princess underwear?" This got Rachel's attention.

"What kind of princess?" said Rachel not looking at Emily.

"Any kind you would like." Rachel did a quick sideways glance at Emily just to see if she was serious about the proposition. "You could get Elsa underwear or Sophia the First?"

"I dunno. Maybe I could get princess underwear and I could use the potty sometimes?"

"No, you need to use the potty all the time once I get you the princess underwear."

Rachel reluctantly agreed to the deal. Emily picked up both children and buckled them into their car seats. She set out to find a store with princess underwear. It was not too hard to find and then they were on the road again. Emily would need to remind Rachel regarding the new arrangement as they did not have ready access to a laundry mat. Rachel did not like being wet, so Emily hoped this was enough of an incentive.

Back on the road the white noise of the tires rolling over the pavement returned with the almost hypnotic effect. One highway blended into another. Towns turning into counties and then finally into states. The closer they were to South Carolina, the greater the evolving dread. It was one thing to be on a frivolous journey but a completely different thing to arrive. Emily decided to stop and stay out one more night before driving to South

Carolina. The accents were slower and thicker, the closer they were to their final destination. The warmth felt good. It was thawing out the reserve Emily typically demonstrated. They briefly had passed by the Smokey mountains which were disarming in their natural rustic beauty. Emily decided to get to North Carolina and make it to Ashton Island in the morning. Emily drove until she made it to North Carolina and stopped at a small town outside of Greensborough. The hotel was clean but simple. There were two queen-sized beds with white muslin sheets and light multicolored quilts. There were layers of paint on the walls and on the door. Some of the paint was chipping at the base boards. The room was painted in pastels and the curtains had a floral pattern which almost matched the faded bedspreads. It had a gentle charm. Emily couldn't help herself from hoping that there wasn't lead in the chipped paint. She would watch both children carefully. The slower pace of things was also frustrating as everything seemed to take longer, from getting gas and checking out at the cash register, to getting food at the local diner. It made Emily feel more on edge. She wanted to get what she needed and then move on. She did not feel like chit chat or listening to others' chit chat. She was feeling increasingly unsettled. She would not allow herself the luxury of reflection or realistic evaluation of her decisions. The fear and guilt were too overwhelming to manage. No, she would go through the new routines of walking, eating, driving and sleeping. Emily could not quite get the last part of the day. She would stay up watching the news or mindless shows, read magazines or low interest books to help distract her brain. She had not checked her phone at these times. The thought of her messages made her feel more apprehensive. She had turned off her notifications and blocked incoming calls. The calls which would strengthen the cord back to realty, back to her old life. She would watch her children sleep with their beautiful innocence and unapologetic snores. This would bolster her for a little longer. Emily wished she could pray in a meaningful way but she felt too far removed from the teenage girl who naively believed that God cared what happened to her. Her unbelief was punctuated with anger. Either He knew and cared about what happened in their lives and allowed it to be so or He did not know or care. Or knew and didn't care. Any way she looked at it, it she could not face going to God right now. Her feeble attempts earlier on the journey she allowed to fade once again. Her heart was too sore. For the time being all, she could do is stave off the panic and dread. She would take care of her small family somehow.

Emily bathed the children and showered. They were getting used to living out of suitcases. She put on an oversized T-shirt and shorts and smoothed her hair into a simple ponytail. She had all three of them on the same bed. She wanted to feel her babies next to her. They were stronger when they were three together. She needed that strength tonight. Emily was not sure why tonight was different. Was it due to being closer to their final destination? Was it due to having to address her decisions and their futures? Was it due to having to face her mother and admit such glaring failure at life? Did this really mean that Luke was gone, and their lives would truly never be the same? Her thoughts would not let her rest. They infiltrated her present and dragged her mind into the churning chaos of possibilities and regret. She would get up and look out the window and then make tea and lie back in bed. She would occasionally drift off to sleep and wake suddenly to her thoughts and panic. She would try to map out the reminder of the trip and even if she went the slow scenic route, it would only take them a few hours to get to Ashton. Emily opened the drawer in the bedside table and looked though the Bible for words of comfort despite her earlier reluctance. After looking though a few scarier verses, she came to look in Psalm chapter twenty, verse one.

"In times of trouble, may the Lord answer your cry, May the name of the God of Jacob keep you safe from all harm."

She felt a little better but uncertain as to why. She put her head again on the pillow and reminded herself that she was strong, and her children were resilient, and people move all of the time. There are single parents all over the country who manage simply fine. Most of whom are not doctors. Emily thought, nor am I any more. Despite this, she was prepared to do whatever she had to do to make a good life for her children. Tomorrow they would meet with their new lives. She finally fell into a sort of restless sleep.

Oliver and Rachel woke her up with a cold cup of water with a teabag and some half-eaten cookies. The cookies that had been laid out by the kettle. "Hi Mommy, we made you breakfast." Oliver smiled proudly as he handed over the tray with the drink and cookie crumbs. "I tried to get the cookies from Rachel, but she kept eating them before I could put them on the tray."

"It is very thoughtful and resourceful of both of you." Rachel had turned away partially in defiance and partially from embarrassment. "I know Rachel would save the best part of the cookies for me. Thank you both for being so kind."

"Well, aren't you going to drink your tea? We added coffee so you would really like it." Emily took a sip and gulped it down. The liquid was cold and bitter with loose tea leaves floating in it. She looked up at both children who were watching her with great anticipation.

"Do you like it, Mommy?" asked Oliver hopefully.

"Of course, I just need to put it in the microwave, so it is warm."

"You said we shouldn't use hot things, so we didn't."

"I know sweetie, I am so glad that you guys stayed away from hot things." Emily quietly poured the concoction down the sink and managed to fill the single serve coffee pot with water and the coffee bag. She went in to the bathroom listening to the gurgling sound of the coffee maker. Emily was energized by the aromatic smell of freshly brewed coffee. It made morning her favorite time of the day. After Emily had showered and washed the children and everyone was dressed, with their bags packed, they headed south towards Ashton Island. Emily reviewed the address. She had typed the address into her phone before they left Minnesota, but seeing the address again reinforced the tangibility of the quest.

"Oliver and Rachel, we get to go to the seaside, doesn't that sound amazing?" They were both engaged in looking at a book which had become lodged between his booster seat and Rachel's car seat. Emily spoke louder to get their attention. "We are going to see the ocean and Grandma." The grandma part was said softly almost imperceptibly.

"Mom, Rachel won't gimmee the book and she doesn't even know how to read."

"Ollie is mean," said Rachel emphatically.

"Okay guys, settle down or the book is mine." These words never solved the problem. They were always met with more statements as to why their sibling was wrong and the desired object should be theirs. Emily knew this when she said those words, but they were one of those automated parental responses. One that you would never believe that you would utter before you had children. She inevitably took the book away and let both of them cry.

Chapter 17
The Reunion

She started down the highway towards the ferry for Ashton. The closer they came the more the smooth roads transitioned to older roads in need of repair and finally to unpaved roads. These roads mostly consisted of compressed sand. They drove to the beach parking lot where the ferry went out to Ashton Island. Emily paid the rough and worn older gentleman and a younger man guided her car onto the ferry. It was a rickety boat, but fortunately it would only be about twenty minutes. Emily looked up the address again and felt panic rising up into her throat. She reminded herself to breathe deeply and to take a drink of water to release the constriction of her throat. They disembarked smoothly and asked where Heron Avenue was located. Google did not seem to be working out here. The roads were barely roads. They were sandy and you could only travel around twenty to twenty-five miles per hour due to their bumpiness. She pulled up at the given address. Emily felt the familiar nausea. Maybe she would not be home. Emily could see an old red car in the driveway. It was a weather-beaten two-story house with a small porch enhanced by an array of brightly colored flowers. There were hanging baskets and tubs in full bloom. The shrubs in front of the porch were neatly tended. The front door was a faded blue, the paint had chipped at the edges of the molding. Overall, the house had a settled and warm appearance. She could just make out the sound of the sea in the distance. Emily got both of the kids out of their car seats. Rachel was impressed with the overall effect and ran to touch the flowers in the tub just at the stairs going up to the front porch.

"Look, Mommy, colors!" said Rachel, more to the flowers than to Emily. Emily walked up the painted wooden steps and took a deep breath and knocked on the door softly. Emily was turning around to leave when the door opened. Beatrice looked greyer but also warmer and softer. She looked at Emily, appearing startled, and then with the largest smile Emily had ever seen from her mother. Beatrice reached out and hugged Emily with so much intensity that Emily thought she would lose her breath.

"Emily!" Beatrice exclaimed. When Emily looked up, she could see her mother's eyes moist from newly unshed tears. "Is this Rachel and Oliver?" All Emily could do was nod. It seemed surreal. The years had been fairly kind. She was still slim and pretty with her sharp bone structure and fine nose. Her skin was tanned and bore the fine lines and coarsened texture associated with aging with the sea and sun. Her hair was mostly white with some of her fair hair still visible, reminding Emily of the beauty of her younger years. Her mother smelled the same, a faint fragrance of peony and bergamot mixed with a subtle unidentifiable scent. "Come in," Beatrice, or Bea as she preferred to be called, said as she welcomed them into her foyer and then guiding them into her sitting room. The room was cozy and functional. It was painted a rich teal which contrasted with the beige and tangerine furnishings. The furniture was comfortable, but threadbare in places. A couple of side tables of teak and mahogany where haphazardly positioned. The overall effect was of a faded Southern charm. Emily was surprised as she had never thought of her mother as 'Southern'. Her mother had spent her childhood in the South, but most of her adult life she had lived in Minnesota. Her stepfather's family were stoic, unassuming Scandinavian stock. Emily's thoughts were interrupted by her mother asking if they wanted tea.

"Um, sure. What kind do you have?"

"I will make some good English breakfast tea; it is very refreshing. I will be back in just a few minutes. Don't go anywhere."

Emily smiled. It wasn't likely that they were going away anytime soon in view their recent journey. "Do you need any help?" Emily offered.

"Oh no dear, you just sit there. I will bring you all out some sandwiches and cakes as well," she said, looking at Oliver and Rachel. They both perked up with the prospect of something sweet. Emily had noted a discernable Southern lilt delicately woven into her mother's speech. It sounded as if it had always been present. Her Minnesota slightly sing-song accent was fading. Beatrice had come back into the sitting room with a tray holding a tea pot, two teacups, two small glasses of lemonade, four small cakes and sandwiches with the crusts cut off. She was trembling when she placed the tray on the small coffee table. The cups rattled as she set it down.

"Where's Luke? Will he be joining you later?"

"Luke is dead," Emily said flatly. Emily looked away from her mother's gaze. She did not want to see the pity in her eyes. Her mother had not known Luke, so how could she fathom what they were dealing with and how great the cavern that he had left behind in their lives? In their hearts?

"Are you our gramma?" asked Oliver breaking the tension.

"Yes, I am your grandma. I am so happy to see you all. I want to know all about you." Bea looked over at Emily and said, "I am so sorry, Emily. I can only imagine how hard this has been. How did it happen?"

"He died in a car crash," said Emily softly. It was the first time someone wanted to know about the details of the event. The event that derailed their lives and lead them to this house.

"I really am so glad that you are here, but I am sad about the circumstances. Did you drive all that way on your own? What about your career? Did you finish your training?"

Emily interrupted Bea from her onslaught of questions. "Bea, I really don't want to talk about all that has transpired over the past weeks. I may at a later date, but now I just need a place to stay with my children. If this is not possible, I will understand. I know this is out of the blue, but I need to know if this is feasible or not."

"You always were straight to the point," said Bea looking down. Emily detected some hesitancy in her voice and was about to round up the children and leave. "Of course, you can stay as long as you want. You and the children will have to share a room. I am currently using one of the bedrooms for storage so we will have to clean it out. You can stay in the larger guest room upstairs."

"It's okay for all of us to sleep in the same room. Thank you."

Bea knew there was a lot to tell but didn't want to push Emily. She was afraid she would disappear out her life again. It had been far too long and whatever brought them to her home didn't really matter. They were there now. Bea silently prayed a prayer of thanks. Bea brought them up to the guest room. It had a queen-sized bed and a single bed, and they were covered by worn floral quilts in colorful turquoise and cinnamon. The room had a large window which revealed a picturesque view of the sea. Emily opened the window which creaked in protest. The aromatic scent of myrtle and the salt from the sea invaded the small room. There was a plain dresser pushed against the wall, above which hung a large ornate mirror. Emily went out to the car to get their bags and went through the laborious task of unpacking.

Rachel looked up at Emily. "Mommy this is pretty. I like it."

Emily smiled back. "Me too, Rachel." This was the start of their new lives. Emily would maybe have time to weave together the threads of the past weeks. Despite this prospect, Emily still felt uneasy. She did not want to go there yet. She did not want to process the events. There was too much dread. Too much loss. Right now, she could see Rachel rifling through the drawers. "Come on, miss nosey, we should go downstairs." She picked Rachel up and went downstairs. Oliver followed closely behind. It felt weird to have other relatives in the same house. Her children felt it as well.

"Mom is she really our grandmother? Oliver asked suspiciously.

"Yes, she really is."

"Do we have a grandpa?"

"No. Not that I know of." Emily went out to the front porch where her mother was sitting on the swing.

"Sit down, Emily, relax. It must be very tiring traveling so far, especially with young children."

"I'm fine. I was just wondering how far it was to the beach. I was going to take the children down to the dock."

"Just beyond those shrubs and striped maple trees." Emily could just make out the beach from the porch. "Why don't you freshen up and I could take the children down to the beach?"

"No," Emily said more forcefully than she meant. It was just that the three of them had become one unit, their own collective. They had survived only because they had each other. Emily could not risk separation. "Sorry, no thank you. I do very much appreciate you letting us stay. I am trying to sort things out in my head right now and I didn't know where else to go." Emily had to look away.

Bea grabbed Emily's hand and looked in her warm brown eyes. "You are more than welcome here; you have always been welcome. I know I could have been a better mother at times and I'm sorry that I hurt you. If I could change the past so you would have stayed in my life, I would do it in an instant."

"Thanks, again," was all Emily could say. She didn't want to go down any more rabbit holes right now. She had to keep herself together to take care of her children. "Rachel and Oliver, come on out here. We're going to the beach." They really did not have appropriate clothes as it was fairly cold when they left Minnesota. They were still in boots and padded coats. She just let them go in their long pants and T-shirts. Emily let Rachel put on her ballerina shoes and Oliver wore his tennis shoes which were too small. She would have to get them more appropriate clothing tomorrow. She looked back at her mother. She seemed more relaxed with the comfort of age. She had a sense of peace that she never had when Emily was growing up. The South and age clearly agreed with her. Emily felt glad that Bea had seemed to get what she had wanted. Emily received her darker coloring and bolder features from her father — so she was told. She had not thought about him for years. Emily only had vague recollections of him from the scarce details disclosed by Bea. The only dad she remembered was her stepdad. The smell of old spice and Scotch. She remembered him asking her questions about herself and showing her the big dipper. Emily thought he must be highly intelligent to know about the stars. She had many more memories of him being angry and drunk. Of his shouting and hitting her mother. Even those memories had faded with time. The emotions seemed to be a far better preservative than her thoughts. In an instant she could be back there as a scared child. Or a child trying to fight to protect her mother. The event could be easily triggered by a strong emotion or threat. Even her nose was more reliable in offering up the past. The scent of summer bringing her vividly back to her childhood. Emily looked at Oliver and she recognized Luke, but she could also see her mother in his face and mannerisms. You cannot escape your genes so it would seem.

Emily led the way through the brush and trees to the sandy beach. The beach was strewn with driftwood and dried seaweed. There were reeds and indentations where turtles would be nesting and laying their eggs. Emily could not remember much about the details of the wildlife in this geographical area. She was a stranger to the South. It felt warm and she could smell the myrtle and sage which was the smell of the sea. She had only experienced this beautiful fragrance on vacation, for brief time periods. The sky had only a few clouds. This was a moment that she wanted to deliberately encode into her memory. Oliver and Rachel were heading down towards the water. At first with enthusiasm but then more tentatively. Emily wished that she had buckets and spades to build a sandcastle, but she was completely unprepared for the weather or the sea. She should have prepared better but she found herself in new territory, where she made it up as she went along. She had taken Rachel's shirt and pants off and Oliver's shirt off. She rolled up the legs on his jeans to allow for greater freedom. They waded in the ocean with the waves pushing them over. Emily was holding on to them tightly. Oliver and Rachel started laughing with the tug of the waves and gentle splashing over their bodies. Emily smiled. She could feel the warmth of the sun and the smell the fresh salty air of the sea. They all three sat down just out of the jurisdiction of the water. The sand was warm and wiggling their feet in the soft golden powder felt exquisite. Emily watched the children chase each other until even they collapsed with fatigue onto the sand. The water was both calming and invigorating. She felt at home with the sea. They made their way back to the colorful front porch. Emily reached to push open the front door but hesitated and then knocked whilst calling out to Beatrice. There wasn't any answer, so Emily opened the screen door and into the hallway.

"Beatrice? Mom?" Emily called out but no answer. She brought the kids up to the bathroom across from their bedroom. She washed their hands and feet trying to clean them up. In the end, she only removed the bulk of the sand with residual grit. She opened the suitcases on the bed and removed their folded clothes. Emily found a lighter dress for Rachel. It was still too heavy but did have a floral pattern. Oliver received a clean pair of jeans and a T-shirt. Emily brushed their hair and combed her own hair and tied it up. They headed back out to the SUV, she would get them more appropriate attire today and not wait until tomorrow. It seemed odd that only hours before they arrived with trepidation and now it seemed familiar and comforting.

Earlier, Emily had asked Bea the directions to the nearest clothing store and found Walmart a few miles down the main road. She caught the sight of numerous unanswered messages. She quickly looked away. She was not ready to face her life yet. She did not know if she would ever be ready. She found the kids section and bought shorts and T-shirts for Oliver and sundresses for Rachel. Rachel wanted sparkly and pink versions of everything. She would settle for Elsa themed clothing but really wanted the rainbow unicorns, which were not available in her size. Oliver didn't really care about the clothing or shoes and quickly agreed to whatever Emily offered. He had his eyes fixed towards the toy section.

"Mommy, could I just see the toys. I miss my toys. I left all my toys in Minnesota." That was the clincher to guarantee going home with a toy. He was really good at this. Guilt was a powerful tool that he was able to wield expertly.

Rachel was more direct about her desires. "I want Elsa."

Emily smiled. "Okay, you can have Elsa." She paid for their treasures and made their way back to the cottage. Emily pulled up in the driveway and brought the bags into the house and made her way upstairs. "Bea? Are you home?" Emily shouted dropping the vestments haphazardly on the bed.

"I'm in the kitchen dear. Where'd you go?"

"We just needed a few things."

"Are you hungry?"

"I am okay, but the kids are probably hungry. I was just going to go and get them dinner."

"Don't be silly. What would they like to eat? I was going to make some crab cakes and corn with biscuits."

"When did you start to cook Southern or coastal or whatever?"

"I have changed in many ways, my dear Emily. Jesus has seen to that."

Emily looked away to hide her discomfort at the statement. "I don't know if the kids like seafood. They are more familiar with hot dish and chicken fingers."

"We'll see, shall we. If they don't like it, you can always make them chicken fingers."

"Okay," said Emily with hesitation. Emily still was not prepared for a relationship with her mother. Especially with her seemingly new persona. Emily had her doubts. She had seen people mimic all sorts of behaviors without a true change in who they really were. This made her slightly wary of the new Bea. Maybe it was wariness of who the new Emily was becoming. She did not know if she could face this journey. She did not know who she was to start with, only who she thought she was. What part she was playing. The suburban mother and wife. The doctor. Competent and loved. The scars carefully concealed. Now she did not know what part to play. She could not stomach playing the poor widow. She could not go back to playing another role. She was free falling. Her only security was her love for her children. They were the reason she had to carve out a new life. The reason she had to continue the journey.

Emily looked up and saw Bea setting the table with Rachel and Oliver. Rachel was very intent on where each person should sit and which glasses to use. She liked the 'fancy' glasses. They were water glasses with a pretty pink floral design. She also wanted the blue green carnival glass plates. The table looked random and colorful. Emily smiled. Rachel was a reckonable force. Dinner was enjoyable with chatter from the children and light conversation. The crab cakes were delicious. Delicately crispy on the outside and moist and light on the inside with saltiness and the sweetness from the crab. Oliver ate two and Rachel had a whole one to herself. They seemed unaware that they did not normally have such fare. Children were amazing. After dinner Emily helped Bea clear the table and wash the dishes and then retired to the back porch for tea. She could hear the crickets and birds calling one to another. Emily sat on the swing with Oliver and Rachel while Bea sat on the chair on the other side of a small table. Emily felt some peace but resisted settling into this feeling. She could not let her guard down at this juncture.

"Come on you two, let's get washed and then to bed."

"Just some more, Mommy?" asked Rachel hopefully.

"Okay a few minutes more."

Bea just watched Emily and the kids. She still could not believe they were there, and she felt that they would vanish if she closed her eyes for too long. Even watching them too hard could make them evaporate. She inhaled deeply and thought, 'my family is home'.

Emily picked up Rachel and guided Oliver towards the door and then upstairs. They were washed and dressed in their pajamas without much protest. Emily put Oliver and Rachel into one bed and got into the other bed. She felt on edge with this arrangement, so she moved the children over and slept with them in the queen-sized bed. Sleep was fitful. Emily was not sure if she would sleep soundly ever again. You can fake being okay in many parts of your life, but your sleep tells the truth. Emily dozed and woke at regular intervals throughout the night.

Morning eventually came. The rays of sunlight illuminating the colorful room. She could hear the birds and the rhythmic whoosh of the sea. The warmth of the sun making Emily sleepy in spite of herself. It was always in the morning when you needed to get up that you felt most like sleeping. Emily remembered that they did not need to be anywhere. This should have been comforting but instead it brought with it the panic of their current circumstances. Emily quickly rose from the bed and headed for the shower before the children woke. She made her way downstairs and saw her mother sitting at the kitchen table with a gooey looking caramel roll and coffee.

"Hi, Emily. Good morning, dear," she drawled when looking up at Emily.

"Hi Bea," said Emily looking away.

"You can call me, mother you know. It's non-comital."

"Of course. I am just getting used to all of the changes over the past weeks."

"Do you want to talk about it?"

"No," said Emily flatly and then softened the response with, "Not yet. I need to figure out where I am with everything, where *we* are with everything."

"It's okay, Lord knows I have had my share of tragedy and change. I know it takes time. I thought maybe you and the children would like a ride on one of the local boats today." Bea regarded Emily's face to see if she could read her story on her fresh unlined face. Whether she wanted to forget with activity or to forget with silence.

Emily shot back. "That would be enjoyable for the kids. What time? I just need to run some errands in town first."

"I can text you with the details once I talk to Noah. Noah is the owner of the said boat. He said he could take us out today. I spoke to him yesterday whilst you were out shopping. I will have to see when he is available and then let you know."

"I am not doing phones right now. I have my phone with everything pretty much shut off. I am avoiding the text messages for now. I could buy a month-to-month phone today. You know 'pay-as-you-go'. Give me your number and I will text you. I will be back in around an hour, two at the most."

"Do you want me to watch the children? It would really be no trouble."

All Emily could think was, it would be immensely helpful as it is tough navigating a life in tatters, and even more so with two kids fighting and distracting one from the practicalities of chaos. However, she could not let her babies be away from her. "No, I will take them to the park in town today. But thanks anyway."

"Suit yourself, I should be here when you get back. If I'm not, go to the marina. Noah is tall with dark hair with a boat called the *Jonah*."

"Thanks, Bea. I'll see you later." Emily grabbed the kids and went looking for a post office to redirect her mail and to talk to her real estate agent. She could also deposit some of the money taken from the drawer before leaving Minnesota. All this and looking around the town for possible jobs. She was feeling tired before these tasks were even initiated.

The town was charming with old pastel-hued Georgian buildings. There was a marina off the downtown area. Several cafes and coffee shops with some second-hand clothing stores. It had a seaside kind of charm: rustic and faded. Designed for leisurely pursuits. Emily was enjoying the feel of the warm sun which was tempered by a cool breeze from the harbor. She caught sight of herself in a mirror walking though the town. Her eyes were sunken and her clothes hung on her reflecting her recent life events. Emily averted her eyes and ran faster with the kids.

"Come on you two let's get you guys to the park."

There was a small park next to the Marina. There were only a few kids playing. Emily remembered it was mid-morning on a Wednesday and that the rest of the world needed to work. She felt a pang of guilt that she was not working. That she had fallen off the ladder, no she had blown up her ladder of success. The years of study and sleepless nights. The financial burden on her and her family all for nothing. She would never be able to afford the two hundred thousand dollars plus of student loans. She could feel her heart pounding with the reality of their situation. She felt as though she was losing her mind some days. She could recite her psychology text books and the counseling that she had given to patients. She knew that she was having an acute stress reaction and in the throes of grieving. It did not help. It just made her feel worse. She should know better but she could not work through the mire. She felt as though she was drowning in quicksand. The more she did the faster she would drown. She would choose avoidance once again. She had become quite familiar with circumvention. A toxic friendship but providing a temporary comfort nonetheless. She had purchased her pay-as-you-go phone and rummaged through her purse to find Bea's number. She located the crumpled paper and proceeded to text her the new number. Almost immediately Bea responded with the time of the boat excursion: three thirty p.m. Emily sighed as it did not leave a lot of time to get the errands run and get back for the boat ride. Despite the rush, Emily was in the mood for further distraction that this offered. She had always loved the water in any case. It was one of the few places where she felt absolutely free. Oliver and Rachel were playing in the sandbox. Both had sand everywhere, in their shoes, their hair, pockets... Emily tried to brush them off to the best of her ability. She picked up Rachel and grabbed Oliver's hand. She belted Rachel into her stroller. Emily had become quite adept at doing things with one hand. She was thankful for the lightweight folding stroller. She remembered the expensive clunky stroller Luke had bought for Oliver; she could hardly move the thing on her own. It was difficult with both of them maneuvering the beast. Experience was an excellent teacher. They would walk the two or three blocks to the post office. Emily loved to walk. It was one of the things she missed most during the harsh Minnesota winters. You could go for walks and most people certainly did walk but it was hurried and a measure of one's character and fortitude rather than for pleasure. Emily also hated the dark evenings and the squeaky snow of January. Something to be survived. To be gotten through. It did make spring all the sweeter. The joyfulness of spring was palpable after an unrelenting winter. And then the buoyant promise of a brief but beautiful summer. Emily likened the process to childbirth, you forget how painful it is until you are in the throes of the process and then forget it again once it is over, until the next time. Minnesotans were hardy, kind people. Emily had simply lost the will to fight the elements. Or the memories. She knew that she would probably regret her decision. One of many. Emily noticed a few disheveled people removing their beds from the sidewalk. She had guessed they were regulars in the area. She saw a free clinic and shelter conveniently adjacent to one another. Her thoughts turned to Iris the addled broken woman. Refuse of humanity. No external value. No wealth or beauty or dazzling brilliance. Yet her presence serves as a brazen rebuke of society. Perhaps this is why it is so enticing to ignore her. To pretend she did not exist. To pretend that she does not matter. To ignore the multiple layers of the system which could have prevented this tragedy: Iris. She had not thought about Iris since her last day at the hospital. She felt a physical heaviness at the treatment or lack thereof of this fragile person. Emily had been another ineffective layer. She hoped that they had been able to save her vision. To be blind and homeless would be too much to bear. Emily smiled at the few worn people sitting on the sidewalk. They mostly looked away or ignored her gaze.

She noticed a 'now hiring' sign in the window of the shelter/free clinic. Her heart jumped at the prospect of working at such a magnanimous facility. People who worked in these places were often the most caring people and, at times, the most unexpected. Nurses working extra hours and looking for something tangible in helping patients or those who had retired from completely different careers lawyers, writers, doctors etc... Those who remember their names and treat them with often long-forgotten kindness and humanity. Light years from the monetary-based models which have inundated health care. And, of course those, who had been in similar predicaments and wanted to give back. Or they just felt more comfortable in the environment. Emily was abruptly reminded that she had not finished her residency. She had taken her STEP 3 and did very well, but no residency completion and no cigar. Why had not she been able to hold it together to finish her residency? Their lives would be completely different. They could have stayed in their community. Among friends and familiarity. Not thrown into this tempest of uncertainty. Panic started to rise in her throat. She could feel her throat constrict once again. She swallowed hard to keep the dread at bay. She held Oliver's hand tighter until he complained and tried to wrestle his hand free. It was difficult to hold on and to maneuver the stroller, so she relented and relaxed her grip.

"Oliver, hold onto the stroller," Emily pleaded. He did so reluctantly. Rachel had her eyes half closed relaxing into the stroller. The bumpy motion lulling her to slumber. She had absolute faith in Emily and where Emily was taking her. Her soft smooth pink skin and messy dark hair made her look angelic. Emily would do anything to protect this beautiful child and this precarious innocence. Life must move forward to provide lives for her family.

Chapter 18
New Life

Emily completed her errands and rushed to the marina with both children in hand to meet Noah and his boat, the *Jonah*. Emily thought it rather cliché, considering his name, but wanted to go out to sea. Also, not wanting to disappoint Bea at such an early stage of their reunification. She was sure that the kids would also enjoy a new adventure. Emily scanned the marina for an inevitable small and worn boat with an equally worn captain. It was Oliver who shouted.

"Grandma, Grandma!"

"Over here!" Bea waved and motioned them over. Emily was not completely comfortable about her children calling Bea 'grandma'. I suppose it was a word that Oliver had not really used before. Maybe he was just seeing how comfortable it felt coming out of his mouth. Bea was obviously pleased by his choice of address and smiled widely. "Noah, this is my grandson, Oliver, my granddaughter, Rachel, and my daughter, Emily. Emily is a doctor, you know."

Emily looked up at this tall dark-haired man with tanned skin and sparkling blue eyes and said, "I'm sorry for that, I was almost a doctor. Currently I am unemployed." His eyes sparkled with an almost stellate quality. She would watch for other signs of a genetic disorder. He did not seem to have any other features of William's syndrome or any other obvious condition. She surveyed him as she would a patient searching for a diagnosis. She smiled to herself. She must have looked more than a little audacious scanning him so intently. She was probably the only person who would think about a disorder when faced with those eyes. In any case, she was not prepared for any bragging about her achievements while her life was such a mess. She just could not manage small talk about anything right now.

"Okay," he said with a warm smile before looking over at Oliver and Rachel. He extended a hand to Oliver to help him aboard. It was an impressive boat with a cabin and artistic calligraphy denoting the boat's name. Emily had not really known much about boats, however, this one seemed to be impressive even by her uneducated standards. After life jackets were secured by all, they navigated out of the marina. Noah seemed expert at traversing the harbor and then out to the open sea. The sun and saltwater felt healing. She kept her arms around both children until Noah volunteered to hold Oliver's hand. Emily reluctantly let go but would not take her eyes off him until she could physically be in contact once again. She could protect him. Their connection corporeal. Emily knew this was extreme, but it did not matter. Her children were her world.

"Look over here, you can see the dolphins."

"Look at that, Mom. Look Mom!"

"I can see them, Ollie. They are amazing."

"Mommy, dolpins," said Rachel, pointing excitedly towards the dark grey dolphins swimming alongside the boat. Noah laughed at the sheer excitement of the children. Emily smiled briefly but was more concerned with ensuring their safety than with their enthusiasm.

Emily looked up at Noah. "Is it common to see dolphins in this area or are we just very lucky today?"

"Dolphins tend to follow the warmer water and food. So no and yes. It helps to know where the good hunting grounds are but as with everything in nature, luck helps."

"What kind of dolphins are they?" said Oliver looking over at Noah.

"Those would be bottlenose dolphins."

Beatrice was watching the interactions with great interest. She was not sure how much she could influence their budding friendship or at least acquaintanceship between Emily and Noah. She did not know Emily herself and clearly Emily was not playing the conventional social games. Bea would leave it to the Lord. She had left many things to the Lord over the past few years. She was getting better at the 'letting go' aspect of this approach. The exchange for this was peace. For now, she would be thankful for her daughter and grandchildren. She would savor each minute.

"Hey Oliver, how would you like to find an island and see if there was buried treasure?"

"Wow, that would be cool. How did you know I liked treasure?"

"I just kind of guessed," said Noah turning the boat towards a small island just off the shore and into the wetlands. They got as close as was safe with the boat and then he dropped anchor and Noah jumped onto the marshy shore. Emily was grateful that she had worn her Walmart sandals and old jeans and T-shirt. Noah reached for Oliver and then for Rachel. Bea decided to stay on the boat and enjoy the sun and she also did not want to interfere with the time Noah would have with her family. She had known Noah's mom from church for the past ten years. Her own mother and grandmother had known his family for generations. His mom died coming up for two years now. She had developed heart failure related to some infection. She died hard. He was good to her and had moved back here from Washington DC for this purpose. His dad had left years before. He had moved to Charleston or somewhere near there. Noah had an important job in the city. He was a junior partner in a prestigious law firm. His mother was so proud of him. She would often talk about her son 'the lawyer' and what a glittering career he had in front of him. Beatrice tried bragging about Emily, but it always fell flat. She felt that she did not have the right to boast. Emily's achievements were hers alone. They only served to remind her of her own failings as a mother. Noah was kind, loyal and smart. He was also a Christian. Bea had learned that these qualities were far greater than his having been a lawyer.

Bea had left when she was a teenager. She could not wait to leave this small Southern backwater where everyone knew each other. To leave the oppressive parenting of her father. The chronic sense of failure, never quite being good enough. Her grades, her attitude, her manners, her appearance. She could not even succeed in holding the affections of her high school sweetheart. 'Sweetheart' sounds too sugary and benign for the intensity their relationship. He had made her feel as if she were worthy and acceptable. Not only acceptable but adored. He was intelligent, not normal intelligent but brilliant and originally intelligent, the kind that could not be taught. He was fearless, beautiful and charming. This affiliation only lasted a season but was breathtaking and all consuming. She had given all she had to this flame, but soon the substrate was consumed, and he moved on to more exotic fuels. She was left pregnant and disbursed. She shuddered to think of her naivety and neediness. This sparked her migration to the North and as far away from Ashton as she could get. Hers being only one of many stories of migration from this town. Once her father died, the beach house became hers. The only home she had ever owned. His family had owned other properties but she imagined that he had sold them or frittered away any wealth. He had done one positive thing for her in leaving her the beach house. This little Southern backwater which had served to hold so many lives, its tentacles far reaching from the respective genealogies.

Her thoughts were interrupted by the distant laughter of her grandchildren. She almost had not dared to refer to them as 'her' grandchildren. She saw the pure joy on their faces. Oliver had a long stick that he was pretending was a sword. Emily kept telling him to stop swinging it or she would take it away. Emily, she was so strong and so beautiful. She loved selectively and fiercely. Bea had wondered the specifics which occurred to bring her back after all this time. She knew it had to be catastrophic, but she would let Emily have her private ghosts. She wanted Emily to know that there would be no failure too great or hurt too deep that would move her to judgement. She knew Emily was proud and did not want to open these wounds. To let herself be vulnerable. Bea wanted to hold her and to help her bear the weight of her pain. She would support her now in ways she could not when she deserved this humanity in the past. For now, she would bide her time and offer her what she needed.

She could hear the clamor of the children and reached out to help Oliver back onto the boat. Emily climbed aboard and grabbed Rachel from Noah. Soon they returned to the main harbor and marina in Ashton. It was late afternoon and both children were complaining of being hungry.

"I know a great seafood place around here if you're interested," Noah tentatively offered to Emily.

"Thank you, Noah, but we should be getting back, I need to give the kids their baths and they are probably getting tired." Both kids protested at the tired comment. Noah looked at Emily for any signs of possible encouragement but found none. It was confusing from her initial apparent interest.

"See you around. Come back if you would like to see more dolphins or treasure."

Emily was already walking away with the children in tow. "Thanks, we will think about it," she shouted back. She did not want to seem unappreciative, but she just could not add any more complications right now, even if they seemed benign.

They made their way home and she made sloppy Joes, chips and salad. No seafood tonight. She walked with Oliver and Rachel down to the beach as was becoming their habit. She would have invited Bea, but she just wanted to be with her children on her own. It seemed to settle all three of them, Emily most of all. This was the remnant of their previous lives.

"Mom, do you like Noah?"

"Sure, Oliver he's okay."

"I like him too," said Oliver looking serious as if deciding whether he was worthy of such an honor.

Rachel looked and shouted, "I like Noah too!" This made Emily feel more uncomfortable.

"Mommy, I miss our house and my friends. Are we going home? Ever?"

"Oliver, I don't know right now. But look, you guys have seen dolphins and your grandmother."

"I know, Mom but sometimes I really miss Daddy and Mrs Lundgren."

"I know sweetie. Me too." Emily walked along the silvery beach with the tide gently slapping over the edge, leaving behind glistening sand. The rhythm being calming. The moonlight making the image ethereal. No one felt a need to say anything else until they got back to the house. They were bathed and put to bed. All three of them sharing the same room until the other bedroom could be cleaned and painted. Emily made a mental note to get that done. Days were developing their own sort of timing. Breakfast and then to the park or the beach.

Several children lived close by and would come by the house with, or sometimes without, their moms. Emily was more than a little surprised by the independence of the local children. They would often go into town at some point in the day and then return to the beach, Emily would talk about the birds or plants and tidal patterns. She enjoyed reading about the specifics of the Carolina coast. The water played a central role in their lives. Emily had not realized how soothing the ocean could be to her jangled thoughts. The water cleansing and therapeutic. It also made her feel connected to something greater. Not alone. She stopped into the homeless shelter in Ashton to see about a job. She had to get some money as her supply was getting low. Emily insisted on paying for groceries and splitting the house expenses. She watched their funds, dwindle to almost nothing. She would apply for more generic positions such as serving food or organizing supplies or accounting. She could apply for lower-level clinical positions, but this would serve as a constant reminder of her failures in her recent choices. Her life so predictable and controlled until it wasn't. She was humbled by the homeless, especially after her own descent. Emily thought about the saying 'By the grace of God go I'. There was not so much difference between the homeless patrons and herself.

She made her way through Ashton with Oliver. Rachel was sleeping and Bea had asked if she could watch her for a while. Emily felt uneasy but she knew it was better for Rachel to stay behind with Bea rather than dragging her out to apply for a job. It would only be for an hour or so. She may not even wake up before she had got back. She walked along the familiar street holding tightly to Oliver's hand. There was the usual group of local indigents lining the sidewalk outside of the shelter. Most looked tired and frayed. She made her way inside the shelter and was greeted with the smell of freshly made soup and bread. It made her mouth water reminding her that she had only eaten half a biscuit that day. The staff seemed attentive and compassionate to their eclectic and eccentric population.

She asked for an application form from a fresh-faced young woman with messy braids the color of cerulean. She smiled and introduced herself as 'Annie'. Emily liked her informal and warm manner.

"I saw the sign outside that said you were hiring. What position is available?"

"General dogsbody. You know serving food, cooking, washing dishes, inventory etc...."

"Sounds busy. Could I have an application?"

"Oh sure, just fill out what type of experience you have and what type of position you're looking for. The pay is not far off minimum wage, but if you have experience, we can maybe go a little higher. You will need to talk to Julie the center manager. She is usually here most mornings from nine to twelve."

"Great." Emily thanked Annie and left with Oliver. It seemed so far from managing patient health and using your brain solving problems, to 'general dogsbody'. At least there were no illusions. It was depressing to think this was the path she was on. The money and hard work and physical hardships had led to this. Emily felt a heaviness in her heart as the gravity of the loss permeated through her mind. She could not avoid this reality any longer. She was unemployed and without references. She was only well trained as a resident physician but without a way of completing her residency at this time. She would work at the shelter until she could figure out something else. It would also serve as a distraction from her failure.

She wanted to get back to Rachel. She felt her heart beat faster. How could she have trusted her mother with her daughter? Being with her children was the only thing that sort of settled her mind and now she was away from Rachel. Oliver seemed blissfully unaware of Emily's turmoil. Emily belted him into his booster seat and got back as quickly and safely as possible. Emily wondered how she would be able to leave her children to go to work.

The sight of the cottage was a relief. She saw Beatrice sat on the porch with Rachel. She appeared to be reading her a story. Rachel seemed content. Emily ran onto the porch. "Rachel, come to Mommy."

Rachel looked up and smiled. "Mommy." And reached out her arms to Emily. Emily picked her up and felt her warmth calm her heart. She squeezed her so tight

Rachel wriggled to get down. "Mommy, Gramma said a good story."

Emily looked at the book. *Goodnight Moon*. Emily had loved that story when she was a little girl. She had routinely read that book to Rachel back in Minnesota. She could hear the distant soothing sounds of the sea. Her children were safe. The panic was over. For now. Their routine of dinner and going down to the beach in the evening was comforting and healing. The clear water seemed to be restoring her soul. Emily would go to the shelter later in the week. She did not feel right about leaving the children just yet.

Days blended one into another. The temperatures soared but were kept in relief near the beach with the cooler breezes coming off the ocean. Beatrice gradually increased her interactions with the children. She was careful not to overstep and constantly checked in with Emily. Emily had steadily relaxed with their living situation. It had been almost a month of living in the South. Emily was meditating on this train of thought, lying in bed with her faded soft sheets and blanket in that blissful phase of sleep and wakefulness. She also thought about Noah. She immediately changed her thoughts to remove him from her mind. She was made fully awake by the loud conversation and laughter coming from downstairs. Oliver and Rachel were already up and in the kitchen with Bea. Emily quickly brushed her teeth and went downstairs. Bea was making pancakes with Oliver and Rachel. Clara from down the road was sat at the mid-century kitchen table taking large gulps of coffee. Her hair was a cheerful red. She was around Bea's age but wore heavy make-up and seemed larger than life. She had dangly earrings which seem to fascinate Rachel. She kept pointing and saying, "Pretty".

"Oh, hello Emily. Did you sleep well? I wanted to let you sleep because I know sleep isn't easy for you."

"Thanks. Uh, yes I slept very well."

"Hi darlin'. Good to see you," Clara drawled as she got up to kiss Emily on her cheek. Emily enjoyed Clara's company, well at least most of the time. She could be somewhat overwhelming given the chance. Clara also attended the same church as Bea which also seemed fairly lively. So far Emily had declined when asked to attend. She was not sure how she thought about God at this time. She felt as if further recriminations were to be had and she just did not want to go there. There was an easiness developing with Bea and the children. More with Rachel as Bea found her sassiness endearing. Oliver was more hesitant and introspective but also starting to thaw. She would have to plan a birthday party for Rachel. Something unicorn themed going by Rachel's favorite television show. Emily had limited their TV exposure but sometimes the need for sanity prevailed and she watched her unicorn show. Her speech was coming on so well. Emily felt pride in how well both children seemed to be doing despite their crazy lives and upheaval. Emily knew to tread carefully and not to take this for granted. Rachel was so smart and intuitive. She had a definitive idea about justice and would battle anyone who she felt was unjust. Emily thought of her as 'Rachel the Lion Heart'. Rachel was passionate about everything. Oliver was more introspective and would calmly weigh evidence in contrast to Rachel's heated approach. He was 'Oliver the Just'. She thought about Oliver's chaotic birthday party after Luke had died. Emily would buy the cake. The pain of that time pierced her heart anew. The realization that Luke was not ever coming back. Their lives would never be the same. This wasn't just a vacation. This was life.

Tonight, was bible study night. They all seemed fairly nice individuals, a kind of motley group. A few were in their thirties, all women, two were well-dressed and the third was rather disheveled with worn joggers and a consistent grey Coca Cola T-shirt, and one young man who seemed to be in his early twenties. He had a full beard and glasses with wild hair. He was tall and lanky with bad skin, from what could be seen. There were two women in their late forties or early fifties, around Bea's age. A couple of ladies in their early sixties. A husband and wife who were in their forties were sickly in their synchronized behaviors and deference to one another. Then there was Clara to complete the set. Emily would find some reason to be out with the kids this evening. Emily was glad for the noise and warmth from the group, but she did not feel ready for the Bible, although she could not deny a tugging at her heart.

She gathered Oliver and Rachel and got into the car and headed for town. They pulled into the marina parking lot. The parking lot was busy. There seemed to be some sort of carnival or festival at the marina. Oliver expressed his approval over the events. He had been bad tempered since leaving the house as he liked staying around the house with Bea and the commotion. He seemed to like being there too much. He did not want to explore the way he did before Luke died. It had been a few days since she had thought of Luke's death and then twice today. Less frequently overall, but just as painful. She hated when these thoughts would sneak up on her and cause her to gasp inwardly. It was almost easier to think about him and the pain all the time.

The afternoon was fading into dusk. The air was warm with the smell of myrtle and the salt from the sea. There was also the fair smells of fried foods and cotton candy. You could hear the twang of a country and western band in the distance and boisterous conversations. They were walking on the promenade taking in all of the smells, sights and sounds. Rachel and Oliver both asking for cotton candy, although Emily could not remember whether they had ever tasted it before. She relented for them to share the pink cloud of the sticky confectionary. Rachel was enjoying the taste and was collecting solid bits of candy on her fingers. She was licking her fingers which did not help with the tackiness. Oliver suddenly started running. "Noah!" Rachel joined in running toward Noah. A man they had only known briefly. Maybe they were really in more turmoil than they let on and seeking comfort in an adult male figure. Noah looked up and jumped off his boat onto the dock and smiled a brilliant smile. It looked more so now. This being due to the effect of his deeply tanned skin, and the reflection from the fading sunlight.

He walked toward Oliver and Rachel and Emily. "It is good to see you all." Looking at each of them and then resting his eyes on Emily for her reaction. Rachel ran to him and reached out her arms and sticky fingers. Her dark curls bouncing as she jumped for Noah to pick her up. He laughed as he gathered her up. "Hello, my girl. What have you been doing?"

"I have the candy," she said proudly holding out her hands with the evidence of her sugary treat.

"I see. It looks like you enjoyed it. How are you? No mother today."

"No, they were having bible study, so we thought it best to escape."

Noah smiled but didn't say anything. "Have you been to the crab festival before?"

"Is that what this is?"

"Sort of an early version. I stopped by your house last week, but no one was there, I had thought of leaving a note, but I really wasn't sure of what to say to you."

"Oh. It was thoughtful to stop by," was all Emily could muster.

"I wanted to see you again, but I didn't want to put you under any pressure. I can tell things must have been rough for you to end up in this town."

"I'm sure my mother must have filled you in on some of the details." Emily said this, but as the words left her lips, she realized that her mother had barely more information than Noah about her life. Emily was surprised at how patient her mother had been.

"Your mother has said extraordinarily little, only that you had come down here from Minnesota after your husband died. She also added that you were a brilliant doctor."

Emily looked down at Rachel's chubby little hands, trying to wash them off with a baby wipe. "What about your descent to Ashton?" she said without looking up.

"Oh, that is a long story and touché." He looked so natural holding Rachel as if he held her like this every day. It made Emily uneasy and she reached for Rachel who reluctantly went to Emily. Emily called Oliver who was walking ahead of them trying to coerce them to go to the ride section. Emily suddenly felt nauseous.

"Sorry Noah but we should really be going. Have a great time at the fair."

Oliver groaned. "Mom! Can't I stay with Noah? I want to go on the rides."

"And me!" exclaimed Rachel.

"Okay two rides each and then we need to go," Emily relented.

"Are you okay?" Noah said with concern, noticing Emily's pallor.

"Yes, I'm fine. It has all been a lot to go through over the past few months. My head is still swimming. I just do not have the energy or stomach for a relationship. I do not want to confuse my children. I do not want, ah... to form attachments when our lives are so tenuous."

"Hey, I am not here to make things worse. I know you have been through so much in a short time. That is why I was hesitant about coming around. Can we be friends? I mean friends. It seems like you could use one about now." He smiled but his eyes still held concern.

"Sure. Just do not be offended if I need to leave or to just back out. Also do not get too close to my children. They do not need any further complications."

"Emily, you are the frankest person I have ever met. I will do my best."

"No. That is the situation. Take it or leave it." Emily gave him a hard stare, so he knew that she was uncompromising with the terms. They made their way to the rides. Rachel and Oliver delighting in the colorful rickety array of carousels. Emily looked up at Noah and softened. "Thanks Noah, I could use a friend."

Oliver and Rachel exhausted themselves with running to the various rides and playing arcade games, Oliver playing and Rachel watching. Time seemed to go so fast that Emily glanced at her knock off fit bit and realized it was almost ten p.m. and way past their bedtimes. She carried Rachel and held Oliver's hand. Noah had reached out to help but Emily's look quickly made him retreat.

"See ya around. Come by the boat when you can. We could do a more detailed tour." Noah said this as he turned and walked away. Emily mumbled something and made her way to her car. She bundled both children into the vehicle . Rachel was asleep and Oliver was nearly there. Emily went to pull out but thankfully looked out the window and slammed on the breaks as a black car pulled out behind her. She stopped and took a deep breath but felt recognizable nausea swell into her throat. She could not quite decipher the make, but it looked familiar. It swerved around the back of her vehicle and out into the unlit road behind the marina. Emily reminded herself that there were a lot of dark cars around and laughed at herself for being paranoid. She drove more carefully and with keener observation in spite of herself. She felt the knot in her stomach relax once they were safely inside and her babies were tucked into the bed across from her own. The porch light had been left on, but she had not checked for Bea, as Emily assumed she must already have gone to bed. Emily had come to rely on the sound of the ocean. The rhythmic waves rolling against the shore. It had become her mantra to feel safe and to lull her to sleep. Unfortunately, her sleep was filled with visions which caused her to wake suddenly. Visions of cars and Luke and the haunting eyes of the man who had broken into their house. It resulted in Emily getting up, making coffee, and sitting on the front porch to watch the sun rise.

Chapter 19
The New Job

"Bea, could you watch Ollie and Rach today? I am going to the shelter to see about the job?" Emily's ready money had all but run out. She did not want to use her account right now. Her crazy paranoia, she thought. She had to arrange Rachel's birthday party and pay her way with Bea. Beatrice had told Emily that she did not need to pay for rent or food, but Emily insisted. It was less complicated this way. Emily should contact the real estate agent or answer her emails and texts, but she felt paralyzed by fear every time she reached for her phone. She had plugged it in several times but could not face turning it on. How far gone was she that she was afraid of a phone. She shook her head and proceeded to talk to Bea. No self-indulgence today. She could hear Rachel and Oliver stirring. Their feet touching the floor, making loud thumps belying their small sizes. They seemed happy. Happier than they had been in a long time. They were comfortable with Bea and the ocean. They had made friends with some local children and were popular with Bea's bible study group. Emily wished she could be settled so easily. She got washed and dressed and got the children ready and brought them to Bea who was sitting in the kitchen staring out of the window.

"Are you all right?"

"Oh, I heard you come down earlier. I'm okay."

"Bea, can you watch Oliver and Rachel while I go to the shelter to see about the job?" Emily enquired .

"Oh, of course dear. Come on you two, I will make you some French toast and then we will go down to the beach to look for future turtle nests."

They barely noticed Emily leaving with such compelling prospects. She went into town and found a parking space fairly quickly. She saw the familiar faces starting their days from the street, gathering their tattered treasures in bags or shopping carts. Emily smiled and wished them a good morning. A couple of the people smiled back. Progress. She saw Annie helping out a frail old lady. At least she assumed she was old, but it was difficult to tell as life on the streets caused one to age rapidly.

"Hi, Annie. I'm Emily. I came in the other day about a job." Emily said tentatively.

"Oh, hi." She smiled a warm smile of recognition.

"Come on over here. Julie will be in shortly." Emily felt relieved. Once Annie finished helping her client, she came over to Emily. "Come on back and I will make some coffee. There might even be some cookies left from the banquet last week." Annie put the coffee pod into the machine until it sputtered the fragrant black liquid. She handed Emily a cup and made one for herself. The cookies were mostly broken but Emily grabbed a larger piece. It was only slightly stale. Emily had eaten far worse in residency. There were two people playing checkers at a table in the back. The clamor of dishes was heard from the staff cleaning up the tables after the breakfast rush.

"So, what did you say you did before?" Annie asked before taking a gulp of her coffee.

Emily hesitated but decided that the truth was the right way to go and besides, she did not have the energy to keep lies straight in her head. Lying was exhausting. "I was a medical resident. My husband died suddenly, and I moved down here from Minnesota with my two children to stay with my mother." You could be truthful without being precise.

"Okay. Do you plan to finish your residency?"

"I don't know right now. I just need a job to pay living money."

"I hear that. There's Julie. She just walked in over there. I will let her know that you are a potential staff member." Annie walked over to where Julie was standing. Julie was a woman in her late fifties with salt and pepper hair and slightly overweight, in a lumpy cardigan way. She seemed kind but more official than Annie. Annie talked in an animated fashion and gestured over to Amy. Julie smiled and invited Emily to follow her to her office. The office was no more than ten feet square with papers and books scattered around. There was an old Dell laptop on her desk. The room had an appearance of vintage chaos. It smelled musty. It did have a window, but Emily had doubted whether it had been opened in years with the layers of dust over the glass.

"So, Annie tells me that you were a medical resident?"

"Yes, I was until a couple of months ago."

"I heard that you have had some hardship recently. I am sorry for your loss."

"Um, thanks," said Emily quietly.

"What skills can you bring to the shelter?"

"I can talk to clients or residents. I can help them apply for services, liaise with social work. Make appointments, clean wounds. I can cook, clean. I can do whatever needs doing. I learn fast and work hard." Emily surprised herself with how much she suddenly wanted this job. To be useful again to others outside of her small family. To be gainfully employed, no matter how limited the amount she would be paid. This would also help to keep the ghosts that haunted her mind at bay.

"Do you have references?"

"No. I kind of burned some bridges when I left Minnesota."

"No criminal record?"

"No. I can emphatically say that I haven't broken the law." Emily thought about the money she had taken before coming to Ashton and looked away. She was not emphatic about anything any more, except she loved her children.

"I think you will work out fine. I will let you know your hours once we get the background check completed." Julie took down her phone and motioned for Emily to leave.

Emily felt like a weight had been lifted on the way back to her car. She looked across at the marina and could see Noah's 'ark', the *Jonah*. He was working on the boat. Emily walked over there without conscious thought, but she felt emboldened by her employment success.

"Hi, sailor," Emily said with her hand over her forehead blocking the sun from her eyes. She always had sensitive eyes, despite them being brown. They were light brown, almost amber, so she did not feel quite so embarrassed about the sun sensitivity.

Noah looked down and a large smile swept over his face. "Hello doc. What brings you to this neck of the woods?"

"I just may have a job at the shelter." Emily smiled back.

"Doing what?"

"Anything they tell me to do. I could work in a shop or an office, but I would rather feel like I was helping people and not just getting a check. The shelter seems like a good place to do this while I figure out my next step back to reality."

"What about going back to medicine?"

"I don't know where I would begin to restart that path. It's complicated." Emily almost told him about the acrimonious circumstances under which she had left her position. She was fairly sure she would not get a good reference from the program. That was killer for her progress in medicine.

"Come on aboard."

"Where are the kids?"

"I left them with Bea. They seem to really like her."

"She is their grandmother, so it helps that they like her," said Noah, smiling ever so slightly. Emily was not sure if he was making fun of her or not. She did not really care either way. Noah helped her up onto the deck. "Do you have time to visit a really cool island known only to a few locals?"

"How long will it take?" said Emily feeling more hesitant.

"Only around half an hour to an hour. You could call Bea and see how the kids were doing or we could all go later."

Emily had already started to punch in the numbers on her pay-as-you-go phone. "Hello, Bea. How are Ollie and Rach doing? Let me talk to them. Hi Rachel, what are you doing?" With a few back-and-forth comments she again spoke to Beatrice. They were looking for seashells to glue onto a frame. She was just about to take them on a play date with some local children who were within walking distance. Bea could chat with their grandmother and they could play on their swing-set. Both children seemed exited by the activity, so Emily agreed and ended the call.

"So, are we going to the island?"

"Sure," said Emily looking up at Noah. She was excited but as ever, pensive. Noah was an expert sailor. He navigated the waters easily with the boat moving swiftly as if going through butter with a warm knife. It appeared that they were going out to open sea, but he turned the 'ark' as Emily now referred to his boat, and she could just make out some trees. He guided the boat to the shore and dropped anchor. The water was shallow, but Emily did not have a change of clothing so was apprehensive about getting wet. Noah offered to carry her to the sandy beach, but she chose to walk, getting her skirt and the bottom of her light blue T-shirt soggy. The water felt warm and soothing. She held her sandals in her hand and begin to relax, to enjoy the feel of the sand beneath her feet. Noah followed close behind. This island had numerous trees, mostly sabal palms, cypresses with a smattering of brush. The sweet fragrance of magnolia Elizabeth filled the air. Emily felt Noah press his hand against the small of her back to propel her forward. In a small clearing she saw a wide array of flowers and an impressive angel oak tree. The massive, convoluted tree was like an enormous awning. The effect was stunning. Emily just stood still and gazed at the magnificent tree and drinking in the intoxicating scents.

"This is amazing," said Emily not taking her eyes off the tree and a large squirrel. She was not sure if she was watching him or he her.

"Come on over here," Noah said as he pointed to where the loggerhead turtles would start nesting in late May. Only a couple of weeks away. How fast and slow time moves.

Again, Emily was aware of the non-linear aspect of time despite what she had learned in physics. It just keeps returning to the past in a circular or spiral fashion, forward and then returning to the past. Until the lesson is learned. She moved to sit on the log under the angel tree.

He sat down next to her but with enough distance for comfort.

"I used to come here when I was a boy. Over the summer mostly. I would work out my problems with exploration. It was one of my few happy places."

"Thanks for taking me here," said Emily not looking directly at him.

"Emily, you have an effect on me that I can't explain. It feels like I've known you forever." He moved closer so he could look into her eyes. Emily touched his face impulsively to remove a gnat and lingered longer than she intended. He reached out to touch her hand and leaned in for a kiss. His mouth pressed over hers. She tasted mint and tea; his tongue was firm and moist. Her heart was racing, and she felt dizzy with sweaty palms. Her body was in acute distress. She wanted to go further. To have him hold her and to feel the caresses and fumblings of new love, but she stopped suddenly and moved away.

"Noah, I can't. I am not going to explain as I already said we could only be friends. I would like to go back now."

Emily was quiet on the way back. "I am sorry Emily. I didn't mean to overstep my boundaries."

"I know, but I thought it was clear that I couldn't handle any more complications."

"I really am sorry; it won't happen again. I would have stopped." He tried to look directly in her eyes, but she averted her gaze toward the netting on board. The rough rope intricately woven to ensnare whatever treasure that could be found. Emily focused intently as if she were going to have to reproduce the complex pattern. They had already reached the marina by the time she looked back at Noah. She thanked him for the excursion and made her way to her car and drove home. The kiss had felt good. Too good. She only lost her husband a couple of months ago. What was she thinking? She had never been the type who could sleep casually with someone. Sex was marriage for Emily, and she knew that fact about herself. She had sometimes envied other girls who could have sex and be over it. No attachments. Emily had always been careful about exposure; you were most vulnerable when intimate. They entered into a private world only seen by those involved. You opened up your heart and your body. The shielding temporarily suspended. She simply was not strong enough to be promiscuous.

When she arrived home, it was late afternoon. The air was already getting cooler. She ran down to the beach to see if she could find the children with Bea. She could just make out three distinct figures. Her family. They seemed to be having fun and Oliver was gesturing in an animated fashion not typical for him. Emily ambled toward them. Rachel was the first to notice and ran to Emily. Emily picked her up and held her tightly and then gently putting her down, holding her small hand. Oliver waved at Emily and ran to show her what he had in his bucket. He had collected a wide variety of shells and rocks from the beach with diverse colors and shapes. He excitedly told Emily about each discovery and his visit to the neighbors and his new friends. He was uncharacteristically lively. All Emily could do was nod and smile with each event told.

After they had dinner, Emily bathed the children and read them their favorite story and tucked them into bed as had become their routine. She got ready for bed herself but slept a fitful sleep. She could not feel settled. She wondered whether she was even capable of sound sleep any more or 'feeling settled', she had only had a few nights of relief before the return of the violent dreams. The visions haunted her slumber once again. The eyes of the stranger more intense and detailed.

Chapter 20
Connections

Emily felt excited at starting her work at the shelter. She would be gainfully employed again. She had just over two months without work, and she felt guilty as if she had been a lazy underachiever. Instead of using the time to create some great revelations or insights. Such as a fabulous career where she could help the multitudes while earning a comfortable income and still have time to be the perfect mother. She barely got through the time without having a complete breakdown and some days she felt this was inevitable and she was holding on tight to just take care of Oliver and Rachel. She would be at work early to run through her tasks. There was no pressure or great expectations at the shelter, which felt unnatural and relaxed at the same time.

Bea had developed close relationships to both Oliver and Rachel. Emily could see the affection growing on both sides. The relationship was different compared to the one they had with Mrs Lundgren. She cared for them but there was not a deep connection. No genetic threads or history to tie them together. Bea seemed connected to Oliver and Rachel. It felt good and frightening. If Bea failed them, it could have far-reaching consequences. Not just a fleeting disappointment. Perhaps it was the openness of their hearts which bound them together, rather than the genes. In any case, Emily was feeling out of her depth.

Today Emily would work from nine a.m. to four p.m. for her orientation. She would work three to five days per week depending on their census and other current needs. Bea would watch the children. She seemed so pleased at being able to spend time with them. Today she had plans for making cookies, meeting with friends, and hanging out at the beach. Emily would not allow them to swim in the ocean when she was not present so they could only hang out on the shore and make sandcastles. Emily was determined to keep her work/life balance shifted towards her children. She also was thinking about looking at her phone and messages. One day at a time.

Emily was familiar with the short drive to the shelter. She parked across the street and walked past the unwashed patrons waking up. She smiled and said, "Good morning", to her new patients or clients as was their preference in address. She made her way into the shelter and saw Annie at the desk. The old building had high ceilings and maroon colored paint with hard wood floors which had seen better days. There were six large cafeteria style tables and an opening into the kitchen via a window in the wall with an area for trays. In the far end of the room were some chairs and a worn couch. There were also a couple of small desks and one larger desk where Annie sat. Emily quickly made her way towards Annie who smiled brightly.

"Hi Emily. Welcome. I will show you where you can put your bag and the refrigerator where you can put your lunch."

"Thanks," said Emily following closely behind Annie. Emily was shown the basics on the kitchen and the inner workings of the shelter. She would help with clean up and getting ready for the lunch. For many of the patrons, lunch would be their only meal. Most of the clients slept rough. There were around twenty beds at their sister shelter, not nearly enough to cover the need. Many had mental health problems and substance use issues. Some just did not have any safety net when they fell and were not able to get back up such was their descent. Some journeys can be extraordinarily harsh. Emily did what she thought was helpful and what she was told to do by staff, some of whom were nearly ten years younger than herself. It was humbling. Kelsey was young and seemed to like this small bit of authority. She had reprimanded Emily for being too friendly with the elderly patrons. Emily liked the clients. They all had stories to tell. Most were thankful for the food and drink and for the company. The smell was difficult to adjust to initially, but Emily put some of her perfume sample under her nose, which helped. The smell of decay and unwashed bodies. Emily saw past this once she got to stop and talk to the diverse customers. The shelter was Christian but not affiliated with any specific church. It felt right being there. Sometimes they would pray with the clients or talk about Jesus, which also served to calm Emily. The hours flew by and Emily looked at her knock off fit bit. It was four p.m. already, she had to get home to see how Oliver and Rachel faired with Bea. Emily excused herself and went to say goodbye to Annie and to get an itinerary for the next day. Julie was sitting at a table in the back by the coats, eating her belated lunch.

"Hi Emily. How did it go today?" she asked with a mouth semi-full of food. She motioned for her to sit next to her.

"Great. I enjoyed helping and talking to the regulars. They are very colorful."

"I am glad you liked it here. You seem to be popular. Just remember to get the work done before the chatting. One of the staff had complained about this today."

Emily felt instantly annoyed but chose to let it go. "Sure, I will remember 'work first, talk later'."

Julie smiled at Emily. "Welcome to the team."

Emily bought two candy sticks from a vendor by the marina before she got into her car to go home. She saw Noah on one of the docks. She quickly looked away and hoped he had not seen her. Before she could pull away, he caught her eye and waved at her. He motioned for her to come over to him, she smiled and shook her head 'no'. She pointed to her wrist and drove off. She saw his number come up on her phone, but she let it go to voice mail. She noticed the car behind her. It was a black Altima with North Carolina plates. She thought she recognized the car for a moment. They stayed at least two cars back, but they kept with her at every turn. She finally stopped and took out her phone to take a picture in an obvious manner in effort to discourage them. The car drove past with a youngish dark-haired man driving the vehicle. He smiled at her and drove on. Emily shook her head. She really must be losing her mind if she thought any Altima plates from North Carolina were following her. Despite chiding herself for paranoia, Emily drove around the island before going back to the cottage. She felt on edge, she was not sure whether this was due to being away from her children or because she was reminded of her unfinished past. She would go to the beach with the soothing water once she arrived home. Water was calming and life giving and right now it quietened her nerves daily. The cleansing pure water.

Chapter 21
Past Revisited

She was relieved to be back to the cottage. Bea was making dinner with Oliver and Rachel. Bea had never been a great cook, but she did not care if you made a mess or if the result wasn't perfect. This made for a fun cook who was perfectly suited for children. They made spaghetti, Rachel's favorite. Emily went upstairs to change before helping in the kitchen. Emily needed to start planning Rachel's birthday party. She would do an informal barbecue with a few kids and maybe Bea's bible study. Emily had limited social contacts in the area so she would invite those quirky individuals she did know. They all ate heartily and the kids both wore more than they ate. Emily cleaned up the kids and then the kitchen. After dinner, they just sat on the porch swing recalling the day's events. The ocean would have to wait. The squeaking of the swing and the gentle breeze creating a comforting rhythm. Emily looked up at the stars and said a quiet thank you. Emily felt a glimmer of hope enter her heart. She scooped up Rachel and Oliver followed upstairs.

"Good night you all," shouted Bea as they were making their way to their room.

"G'night Gramma," said Rachel. Oliver had already gone into their room.

Days were going surprisingly smoothly except a few minor exchanges with Kelsey at the shelter. Emily was becoming proficient at the intake and feeding large numbers of people and quick clean ups. She was also able to help them with paperwork to get health care coverage and advocate for them to get on housing lists. There were still so many barriers, but she was learning to take things day by day. Emily was developing friendships with a few of the regulars. Morris who was cranky and brusque in his interactions, had been a math teacher in a former life. It was hard to imagine him being social enough to work with children, but apparently, he was good at it. He had a plaque from the school honoring him as 'Teacher of the Year'. Emily had noticed it in his bag of treasures. After the death of his wife from cancer, he gave up. He spent his days drinking and then lost his job and eventually everything else. He says he did not really care about the material things as nothing could, "Replace my beautiful Shirley". They did not have any children to keep him, so he just let go of the reigns. Free falling. His journey rambling and then crashing. He enjoyed playing chess and beat Emily with regularity. He seemed to take more than a small pleasure in doing so. Emily had also noticed that he had a weeping wound over his left forearm. Emily had asked about the wound repeatedly, but he would not let her look at it closely. She had only seen glimpses of what looked like a cellulitis or an abscess or both. He said he could not recall how it happened. But it had been, "Over a week ago". He would not go to the clinic because he, "Hated all doctors". Emily convinced him to sit tight and went over the free clinic next door, asking for a wound kit and whether they had any antibacterial ointment. She also asked if they had any Keflex or clindamycin.

The doctor came out to talk to Emily. "Hi, I am Doctor Roberts, how can I help you?" Emily went through Morris's history again. "You talk doctor, what's the story?" Emily succinctly explained her current situation. He smiled and said, "Welcome to the world of homeless medicine. I may need your help around here sometime." Dr Roberts was in his mid to late sixties Emily guessed by looking at him and by the dates of graduation from medical school and residency. These dates reflected in his degrees framed on the wall. He went to Princeton medical school, a good Midwest university for his undergraduate studies and he looked kind. Emily's favorite kind of doctor, smart and compassionate. The waiting room was full of patients waiting to be seen so he agreed that she could have the wound kit. He would need to see the patient for the oral antibiotics and would stop by the shelter at lunchtime to see Morris. One of the nurses, Kerry followed Emily to the shelter. Emily was relieved and grateful for his generosity. She knew how difficult it was getting through a schedule and the time it took to leave for one patient. You could see at least four patients in the same time period. She liked Dr Roberts.

Back at the shelter, Emily agreed to give Morris extra dessert and ten dollars to allow her to dress his wound. She expertly exposed the area. There was a three centimeter by five centimeter area of erythema and induration over the forearm with a central sinus. She washed the area with antiseptic soap and water. She needed to do this twice to allow the water to run clear from the dirt over his arm. Kerry offered to do the procedure as this was what Dr Roberts most likely had in mind. But Emily declined and proceeded to expertly inject the wound with lidocaine. Once numb, she drained the abscess with a sterile scalpel included in the kit, although this was technically a 'dirty' procedure. This meant that items should be clean but not necessarily sterile. The lesion drained around five milliliters of purulent fluid. The wound was too shallow to be packed with a sterile swab. Emily cleaned the area again and then squeezed the Bactroban over the area. She had him stay until Dr Roberts could see him.

Kerry went to get Dr Roberts when she saw him make his way into the shelter and was directed over to Emily by Annie. Dr Roberts looked over the area. "The wound looks good, but I agree he needs clindamycin for the next week. Thank you, Kerry."

"Um, Emily did all of the work," she said looking away, hoping he wouldn't be angry that she had allowed Emily to carry out the procedure.

"Thanks Emily, great job," he said looking towards Kerry with a reassuring smile. It felt good to be using some of her skills again. To be part of the medical profession again, no matter how small her role. Emily gave Morris ten dollars a day to come back for the wound to be assessed over the week. Fortunately, it healed without incident. Morris started eating better and seemed happier overall. This could not be completely explained by the wound treatment, but Emily was not going to question this change as she was enjoying his new-found positive demeanor.

Emily helped Dr Roberts out on occasion, to help with getting a history or even as a second opinion. She would need to get credentialed to do more hands-on patient care and he pushed her to move forward with the process. She could not face this yet. She continued to help with the patients at the shelter but was again told to refrain from medical interventions. She could dress simple wounds there but would need to send them to the clinic for deeper cuts and other medical issues. She resigned herself to these minor procedures. There were new clients coming into the center daily, both young and old. Increasing numbers with substance use issues. They all did what they could to help with their limited resources. Emily was well liked and usually handled the intakes.

It was a busy morning with new clients pouring into the center. Most wanting food and a place to hang out, but a couple also needed help with forms. Emily was helping Morris with his forms for Medicare, when she was abruptly interrupted by shouting.

"I know you. I know you. Hey you. Hey you. Sorry about Luke." With that Emily turned around hastily to see a scrawny woman in her mid- to late-twenties with dirty blonde hair, calling out to her. "Ain't you Luke's o'l lady?"

"Who are you?" was all Emily could say. She looked vaguely familiar, but Emily could not place her.

"I'm Boo." She said slowly. "My real name is Elizabeth. Elizabeth Wallace, but everyone calls me Boo. I knew Abby." She smiled with her yellowed teeth and seemed to be looking at something fascinating on the wall. Emily thought she remembered her from one of the photographs at Mrs Lundgren's house. She was posing with Abigail at the beach.

"How is Abigail?" Emily asked not sure of where to go with the conversation.

"Abby's dead. Dead, dead, dead. Like a door nail." Then Boo started laughing.

"What? How?"

"She got some bad 'poppy' in Greensboro."

"When did this happen?" Emily said feeling nauseous.

"I don't knooow." She was slurring her words even more and was no longer making sense. "Help me. I know I am baaaad, I just don't want to be dead, dead." And then drifted off without completing the thought.

Emily looked at her eyes. She had pinpoint pupils. Her respirations were slowing, and she was confused. Emily called out to Annie, "Get an ambulance, now! Is there any naloxone here?"

"I don't know. What is that?"

"It's an antidote for opiate overdose." Emily called out to one of the other staff to get Dr Roberts from next door. Emily had already started the CPR assessment. Boo was barely breathing, and Emily had started breathes when the ambulance arrived. They gave her a shot of naloxone and got her onto the cot and into the ambulance. "See you Boo," Emily said quietly as the ambulance pulled away.

Dr Roberts had appeared as she was being taken away. "What's going on?" Emily recounted the events. "It sure isn't boring around you. Thanks, Emily, for your quick thinking."

Emily was aware that she was shaking. She was thinking about Abby and this strange interaction with Boo. "Are you okay? Emily?" asked Julie who had rushed into the main area with all of the commotion.

"I think so?" answered Emily still visibly upset.

"Come and sit down." Julie motioned towards the chair by the main desk. "Have some water."

"I'm okay, really," Emily said regaining her composure.

"I think you should go home. You have dealt with enough today," Julie declared softly but firmly. "Are you all right to drive?"

"Yes, I will be fine." Emily managed a weak smile to reinforce the sentiment. Emily gathered her things and made her way out into the bright sun and towards the covered area of the parking lot. She did not feel like going home just yet as she needed to process what had just taken place. She found a bench in the shade and just sat. She could see the marina and the 'ark'. She got up and made her way towards her only friend in Ashton. She could see Noah moving boxes onto the boat.

"Hi Noah," Emily said before she thought it through.

He looked up and waved to Emily. "Hey come on over." He smiled his most convincing smile. Emily just sat with him on the boat while he recounted his day and the contents of the boxes. He could tell something was wrong but did not want to spook her again. "Let's go get some tea." Emily agreed as they made their way through the marina. She was getting used to the sweet tea of the South, but still preferred the un-sugared variety of the North. He asked about the shelter and she relayed some of the amusing stories from the patrons. Their conversation felt comfortable. He listened intently as Emily briefly told him about her day and the naloxone. She left out Boo's connection to her life in Minnesota. She wasn't sure why. But she just did not want to go into any further details right now.

"Emily, I am really sorry about before..."

Emily cut him off before he could finish. "It's okay Noah, I am just not ready for that kind of a relationship right now. I am glad to have you as a friend." Emily felt a fluttering in her stomach around Noah, but she would suppress her feelings for him at present. Emily briefly hugged him, said goodbye, and made her way home. Emily noticed the black Altima across the street. The North Carolina plates just visible. She had just turned her car around to see if she could find the owner of the vehicle, but the car had already gone. Maybe it was a mirage.

All she could think about on the way home was Abby and Mrs Lundgren. Emily felt sorry for Mrs Lundgren, she could not imagine the pain of losing a child and an only child at that. She wondered if she had called her, but her phone had been shut down. She would need to go through her messages. At least some of them. This task could not be put off forever. She decided to embark on this task today. The drive seemed quicker than usual, due to her clouded thoughts.

At home Oliver and Rachel were both playing with a neighbor's dog. Oliver reminded Emily about her promise of a 'olden reliever' dog. Emily smiled; kids never forget the promises. He could not remember to put his clothes in the hamper, but he would remember promises made in the throes of grief. They would look for a dog. Beatrice seemed relaxed and readily agreed to a dog.

"Hi, Emily. So good to have you home. How was work?"

"Fine. How was your day?" Emily listened with delight with regards to the adventures had by them. They had been careful at the beach not to disturb the turtle nests which would be starting to occur. Oliver had collected an impressive array of stones and shells. He could identify them all. Rachel played with neighbor children and ate refreshing watermelon. They would have her party the following Saturday and Rachel had recited a list of things she would like for her birthday. Despite the domestic harmony, Emily's uneasiness returned. She enjoyed the evening with her children and with Bea. Both children seemed to relish their days and slept soundly most nights. Emily was thankful for this and envied their sleepy innocence. She just couldn't shake her unease, especially with Boo, and Abby dying.

She planned to review some of her messages and then go and see Boo at the hospital tomorrow. In the morning, Emily was awake at first light after another restless night of choppy sleep. Emily grabbed a coffee and went to sit on the porch with her phone. There were numerous calls and messages from Amy and a couple from Ashley. She saw a few messages from the real estate agent and insurance company. This was going okay, this was doable. She did not recognize the numbers or voices for a few of her messages, but the sound of one of the voices sent a chill down her spine. The voice asked for 'Luke Wilson'. There were several calls from the sheriff's office asking her to return the call and one from the coroner's office.

She decided to call the coroner's office. The receptionist took her information and said she would have the coroner call her back. The sheriff's department transferred her to Sherriff Olson.

"Hi, Mrs Warrington?" she asked hopefully.

"Yes."

"We have been trying to reach you."

"Oh, I went to stay with my mother in South Carolina."

"We managed to track you to a 'Bea Reynolds'' residence in Ashton, South Carolina. We were trying to get a hold of you as there was a break in at your home in Plymouth."

"I know I reported this before I left."

"This occurred a week after the initial complaint, your phone was tracked to be out of state during the occurrence. It was reported by a neighbor. The house was also set on fire."

"What?"

"The house had been set on fire," she said flatly.

"Was anyone hurt? Who could have done something so awful?"

"That is what we are trying to figure out. Have you noticed anything out of the ordinary recently or know of anyone who would try to hurt you or your family?"

"No."

"What about for illicit drug use? Mr Warrington's blood was positive for opiates from the coroner's report. High levels of opiates, mixed with a few other substances."

"I can't believe Luke would do this." Even as Emily was saying this out loud, she knew this made perfect sense. The lies, the money, the association with Abby. "This could be coincidence, but I have seen a black Altima, it looked to be the same car I saw in Minnesota when my house was broken into. It had North Carolina license plates, I didn't get the number, but it looked like the same vehicle. I also saw someone named Elizabeth Wallace or 'Boo' who knew Abigail Lundgren or Green who also had substance use issues and was close to Luke. I think she said she was living in South Carolina, but had come from Greensboro, North Carolina. I have been working at the local shelter and she came in yesterday very drugged up. She needed to be given naloxone and admitted to the hospital in Myrtle Beach."

"Mrs Warrington, it would be helpful if you could go to the FBI field office in Myrtle Beach to provide this information to them as this is now out of our jurisdiction. An Agent Osborne should be able to help you in that office. You need to go there today." Emily had the feeling that she knew a lot more than she was telling her. She was not surprised with any of Emily's disclosures. She felt a little like bait.

Emily called the hospital in Myrtle Beach and Elizabeth Wallace had left AMA this morning. Emily went into the kitchen where Bea was making a smoothie for breakfast. "Hi, honey, I saw you on the porch, but it seemed like you were dealing with things, so I left you be. How's it going? I can help, Emily. You don't have to do everything on your own," Bea said looking into Emily's eyes.

Emily turned away. "Mom, could you watch Oliver and Rachel today so I can go over to Myrtle Beach. There are a couple of things I need to deal with?"

"I would but, I have to rehearse over at the church for our choir concert tomorrow in Charleston. The churches are coming together for a radiate conference. Would you like to come?"

"No Mom, but thanks." Emily had only just started calling her 'mom', it felt fairly natural and Emily could see the pleasure on Bea's face with this change. "Okay, I will get the kids up and take them with me today." They both got up relatively easy and once breakfasted they headed out to the car. They reached Myrtle Beach in good time. Emily parked in front of the nondescript building on

Mayfair Avenue across from a BI-LO. It looked more like a suburban strip mall than a government agency. She brought both children with her, holding their hands tightly. The receptionist appeared uninterested but mildly disapproving of having children in the area. Emily asked for Agent Osborne. The receptionist called back and a few minutes later, an officious looking man in his forties or early fifties with sharp bird-like features and a neat blue suit appeared. He introduced himself to Emily and to Oliver and Rachel. He extended his hand to Emily.

"Hello Mrs Warrington or Doctor Warrington." He said this to inform Emily that he was aware of her history. They had obviously excluded Emily from the perpetrator group by his demeaner. Emily went through all that she knew and gave him her phone so he could listen to her messages. He made detailed notes of their interview and recorded the phone messages of the unknown voices. He had reviewed the phone numbers and told Emily to come back if she could recall anything else. He also placed a chip in her phone should these unknown callers try to contact her again. He gave her his card. He said that they were interested in drug cartels from the Carolinas; they were increasing their territories. When Emily discussed Abigail, he seemed to already know her association to Luke, although Emily was not quite sure of their relationship herself. It was disorienting. He also knew about her demise.

"Are we in danger?" Emily asked, suddenly feeling apprehensive.

Agent Osborne looked at her directly. "We will do all that we can to keep you safe, just contact us with any new information. By the way, Doctor Warrington, we did find opiates in your home, in brown packages that we were able to salvage. We don't know if that was what they were looking for or something else? We also checked your DEA prescribing history, which was clean, by the way."

Emily was trying to process all of the information. Rachel and Oliver were playing with Agent Osborne's replica of the USS California. "Hey, you guys, put it back," Emily said louder than she had intended.

"I have kids. It's okay."

"What else would they be looking for? Who are they?"

"We thought you could help answer these questions."

"I don't know about any of this. I went to work and came home that's all I did. I thought Luke was working as an accountant." Emily started to get upset and Oliver and Rachel stopped playing with the ship and rushed over to Emily and put their hands on her shoulders.

"Mommy why you sad?" asked Rachel giving Agent Osborne as menacing look as she could muster.

"It's fine Rach," Emily said smiling at her.

"We know this, Doctor. We can account for your whereabouts. We just want to know if you know anything or remember anything that maybe helpful to our investigation. Please call me with anything."

"I will, thank you, Agent Osborne," Emily said still shaken from the revelations.

"Oh, and Doctor Warrington, don't discuss this case with anyone. We wouldn't want to let any of this information get out as that could be dangerous for everyone." He had dark brown almost black eyes and maintained eye contact uncomfortably to bring home his point.

On the way home, Emily remembered the call when they were on vacation from a Tony Duplantis or Dupont. And that he had called for Luke Wilson and Luke had left shortly after this and seemed upset. She called the number on Agent Osborn's card.

"Hello, Emily, how can I help?" She recanted the events. "Are you sure he said Tony Duplantis or was it Dupont?"

It was clearer to Emily now that she had triggered the memory. "It was Dupont. Definitely Dupont."

"Why didn't you say this before?"

"I just thought of it now. I didn't know what was going to be important at the time."

"Well this could be important. Thank you, Emily. Be careful."

On the drive home, Emily allowed them to watch the latest Trolls' movie to help organize her thoughts and to try and make sense of the information. Her brain was hitting overload. They went home ate dinner followed by the beach. The beautiful water refreshing Emily and helping her with clarity. The peace of the water restoring her heart once again. Neither child asking about the visit to the FBI. Maybe they did not want to know how easily life could be changed again. They wanted the comfort of the developing routines and familiarity. That night they both slept with Emily.

Chapter 22
Sins and Redemption

Emily left for work. Both children were still asleep, lying comfortably entwined with soft toys and each other. She briefly waved to Bea as she went out the kitchen door. Bea would get them their breakfast later. She would need to get home by four thirty p.m. so Bea could get to Charleston for her 'radiate' conference. Emily did not feel a significant softening with regards to reconciliation with the Lord. She was still angry about Luke and, now that he was gone, that he had put them all in danger. Oliver and Rachel were so innocent. Emily just could not open herself up any more to anything. There was increased traffic today which forced Emily to park on the far side of the marina and she would have to pay for parking. She would have to move it at lunchtime. She felt excited in spite of herself, that she might see Noah. She wanted to tell him everything, but she could not involve him, involve anyone. The sense of isolation had returned with the recent events. Emily was also feeling some of the old guilt with trying to navigate working with parenting. Bea had helped tremendously, but she still did not want to miss any part of their lives. However, money was also needed, such is life.

Surprisingly, the day went without hiccup. At lunch, she moved her car and walked over to Noah who was sitting on the dock. He seemed serious, but happy to see her.

"Hello doc."

"Hi counselor."

"I prefer captain," he said with a flicker of pain flashing across his eyes. She knew there was a story behind this reaction. She would address this another time

"Okay captain counselor." He smiled and motioned her over.

"Do you want to get some lunch?"

"Sure, but I only have twenty minutes, so it needs to be quick." They found a fish and chips shop, the marina's version of fast food. Emily still hadn't developed much of a taste for seafood, so she just had the 'chips', or French fries with vinegar. They were crispy on the outside and velvety soft on the inside with the saltiness and tang of the vinegar. There were other subtle flavors from the seasoning and oil, but they blended seamlessly to create a delicious treat. Emily had her unsweetened iced tea to wash it down. She felt lighter being with Noah. His eyes were sparkling, but she no longer considered a possible genetic disorder when looking into them. She smiled to herself about her previous thought process, maybe she was the one with the disorder. Emily did feel as if she could lose herself in the depths of his eyes. They were tender and unfathomable. She knew that he also had pages in his story that he would prefer to encrypt or that he would like to tear out, but overall, he seemed happy with his journey. Unlike Luke. Noah had been coming to the cottage with regularity to see Emily, Oliver and Rachel.

She looked up at Noah as he touched her hand and then her arm but was careful not to linger and to watch her expression for signs of discomfort. She was feeling more at ease with him. He was her friend. She wanted him to become more than her friend, but not now. She did have his number on her phone as a contact although she had not called him and probably never would. She finished her lunch and hugged him briefly but lingering just a little longer than needed.

"Emily, I enjoy seeing you. I just want you to know that you can tell me anything. I may not have a great answer, but I am prepared to listen. I have been known as 'counselor' in the past."

She smiled at him. "Thanks Noah, I am enjoying seeing you as well. I will keep that in mind. The talking part." She hastily grabbed her bag and walked toward the shelter without turning around.

She finished the rest of the day seeing mostly the regulars. A steady stream of paperwork and helping out in the kitchen. She was doing less of the kitchen duties as Julie wanted to utilize her skills in advocating for the clients. She was able to get most of the usual clients on some sort of Medicaid or Medicare and on shortlists for housing. No small feat. Emily had helped clean up and left for the day feeling satisfied with the progress that was being made for her clients. She got into her car and drove home. She enjoyed driving on the coastal road. The water glittering in the warm sun, was salve to the soul. She could tell that her shell was gently being chipped away. She would enjoy having the house on her own, with her children. She might even invite Noah over for dinner.

When she arrived home, Bea was in a hurry to get out of the house and pick up a few of the other ladies in the choir. Bea picked up her suitcases and placed them in the car and came in to get her purse. She saw Emily in the doorway. She took Emily's face into her hands.

"I love you, Emily, and I love the children. I am so blessed that you were brought back into my life." She then turned and walked out the door. Emily was amazed with her mother. She had really changed. How had she been able to change her journey's direction so completely? Emily was feeling thankful for this transformation. She may not have known the new Bea if the events of her life had not led her to the cottage. Why did it have to be so hard to gain this relationship? People will often express gratitude for the smallest success after sometimes catastrophic events. Maybe it was because without this, the sadness would be unbearable. Or if your eyes were opened to the beauty and kindness present In the background of everyday. Emily was not sure if any events in life were related. Or just a collection of random coincidences, which keep us ceaselessly on the ropes.

She could hear Rachel and Oliver playing upstairs. They were arguing over which shell was better. Emily called them both down. "Hi guys, how would you like to go out for dinner?"

"Somewhere fun?" asked Rachel.

"Yep. Somewhere you would both like to go." Emily wanted to take them somewhere special. It had been a few weeks since they had gone out for dinner. She drove over the bridge out of Ashton and headed for a local waffle restaurant a few miles down the coastal highway.

"Mom, I love waffles!" said Oliver when he saw the sign.

"Me too!" Rachel chimed in. Emily smiled and helped both kids out of the car. It was good to spend time together just the three of them, although Emily vaguely missed Bea. It is crazy how bonds form and re-form just by proximity and necessity. They all ate well. Rachel and Oliver were engaged in lively conversation.

"Mommy, when is my birthday party?"

"Next weekend, sweetie. We will have unicorn cupcakes. We will invite Ellie, Marley and Jonah and the people from Grandma's bible study. It will be so fun." Rachel would have Emily repeat the details of her birthday party over and over. She became more exited with each telling.

"Rachel, you know about your party," Oliver said getting frustrated with the retelling.

"I can heard it again if I want."

"Hey you two."

"Mom, my birthday wasn't very good," Oliver said looking down.

Emily felt her stomach wrench. "I am sorry honey; I just didn't have a lot of experience making cakes."

"No, that's not why. It was bad because Daddy wasn't there," said Oliver looking down and moving the chunks of syrupy waffle around his plate with his fork.

"I am sorry Oliver. I know it has been so tough on you guys. I know you have missed your dad. How are you doing now?" Emily did not believe in treating children like babies. She wanted to know how they were processing all that they had gone through.

"I feel sad sometimes but not as much any more," said Oliver.

"I am glad sweetie. Is it okay being with Grandma?"

"Yeah, I like Grandma, but not her cookies," added Rachel thoughtfully.

"I like Grandma too. I also like my friends and the water. And I like you being with us. And Noah."

"I love being with you guys too. You know that you can always tell me anything okay? Even if you think it will make me sad or mad. Do you know that? I will always take care of you."

Oliver was looking bored by the end of the conversation. "Okay, Mom. Can we go down to the beach when we get home? I want to see the turtle nests and get some more rocks and shells."

"Okay, kiddos." Emily paid the bill and they headed back for home. Turning onto the highway Emily saw a glimpse of what looked like the black Altima in the parking lot as she left. She could not quite make out the license plate from the partially obstructed view, but it looked like the same vehicle. She reassured herself that Agent Osborne would have checked out the car, they were the

FBI after all. They pulled up to the now familiar house, it was dark except for the front porch light. They made their way through the front door. Everything as they left it. The shoes in the entry way and the keys haphazardly placed in the dish by the door. Oliver wanted to get his bucket and shovel before going down to the beach. Emily grabbed a couple of towels and then they all headed down to the shore. The beach was fairly quiet. It was that time just before dusk when there seemed to be a tranquil quality to the sea. Fewer crowds and just the sound of the rhythmic waves caressing the shore as they have since the beginning of time. Oliver and Rachel had come to regard the beach as their favorite playground. Emily threw her towel down with her phone wrapped in it. She threw it next to a collection of rocks further back from the sandy beach area. Oliver and Rachel were both looking for frogs in the small pools of water by the rocks. Oliver had found a few interesting shells. Some with irregular edges and a kaleidoscope of colors over their outer aspect and a couple large shells with more uniform color formations. He seemed particularly proud of these finds.

She was more amazed with her children as the days went by. They had survived so much and were thriving. They loved the routine and family. Her thoughts were interrupted by two distinct figures coming toward them from the distance. There were only a few other people around who were in the far distance, walking their dogs. Emily immediately felt uneasy. She looked over at Oliver and Rachel who were still playing in the shallow pools away from the shore. The figures were two men, possibly in their forties, wearing heavy long coats which were clearly inappropriate for the weather.

One of them pointed towards Emily and shouted, "Emily?"

She shouted back, "Who are you? Why do you want to know?" She was moving away from the shore and towards her children as she was speaking. She felt her brain go numb. She suddenly recognized one of them from the black Altima. His eyes had been familiar and suddenly remembered them as being the same as the man who had broken into their hours in Minnesota. Quickly coming back to her senses, she shouted, "Oliver and Rachel run home. Go now or you both are going to be in trouble! Oliver call nine-one-one on my phone. Now! Run!" They didn't question the command and started to run. They could sense the seriousness of the situation, even at their young ages. Oliver held Rachel's hand tightly as they made their way through the brush and onto the sandy driveway and, finally, into the cottage. They had left the door unlocked and thankfully, it was slightly ajar. Once inside, they both became aware of how fast they were breathing.

Rachel started to cry. "I want Mommy."

"I know Rachel, but we have to be big right now." And then hastily added, "For Mommy." He called nine-one-one and said his mom was in trouble on the beach. He didn't know where, but fortunately they could trace the call. He remembered Noah and how he made them feel safe. He looked for an 'N' on the phone. He found it and called him.

Noah had to glean what happened from Oliver's choppy recollection of the events. He could hear Rachel crying in the background. "Oliver, you did so well. Thank you for taking care of your mom and Rachel. Let me talk to Rachel. Rachel this is Noah I am on my way. Everything will be okay. Oliver will take good care of you." He spoke to Oliver again and advised him to take Rachel upstairs and to get under the bed until he got there. Like a hide and go seek game. Oliver agreed. He felt better after talking to Noah.

Noah called the police again with specific location details for the beach and the house. He also called a neighbor, Orleen, to go and get the children and bring them to her house. He just wanted to get to Emily and the children. He did not particularly like guns, but grabbed his Smith & Wesson 351 C. He loaded the gun and put it under his seat in the car. He could not imagine hurting someone, but he had to protect his new-found family. He started to pray like he had never prayed before. He was feeling some peace when he arrived at the house.

Emily now moved toward the distant figures on the beach. She could see Oliver and Rachel disappearing in the distance as the men started to pursue her, steadily catching up. She tried to run towards the distant figures walking their dogs. When she felt them gaining on her, she turned around to face them.

"What do you want?" Emily was breathing fast from her attempt to get away and from fear.

"You know what we want," the tall dark-haired man from the Altima said.

"No, I really don't. I am just trying to take care of my children. I don't have any idea what you could possibly want from me."

The larger of the two men moved to grab her arm. He clutched her left arm with his large stubby fingers digging into her flesh. "Come on and we will explain it on the way," he said this with a sadistic smile. "Luke enjoyed our company. So did his girlfriend. You remember Abby, don't you?"

The Altima man said, "Enough with the games. We want the ledgers and brown packages you brought here from Minnesota. Luke was very detailed in his work. We know you brought them here because we searched the house, and they were gone. Come on, Doc, give them over and we may let your kids live."

Emily felt panic rise up in her. She saw Oliver's bucket on the beach just past her right foot. She reached down and threw the wet sand and shells at the larger of the two and hit him in the head with the metal bucket. She screamed as loud as she could to momentarily catch them by surprise. The larger one shouted as he tried to get the sand out of his eyes. She started to run, but the Altima man grabbed her by the hair and pulled her back. She would not stop screaming. She tried clawing his face and jamming her fingers in his eyes. She was trying to remember physical vulnerabilities from her anatomy knowledge. She felt stronger fueled by her adrenaline and then need to get to her children. She tried kicking him in the genitals and pounding on his chest to stop his heart. The stockier man punched her on the side of her face. She felt the impact and immediate pain and swelling as she went to the ground. She knew she had to get away and tried again to get up and run. She could hear people shouting. She kept screaming and was able to get up and run. She was thinking that she might actually get away when she heard a loud cracking sound and felt sharp burning pain in her back and then in her abdomen. The pain was hot and searing, which took her breath away. She saw the blood flow onto her white T-shirt. The blood appeared as vermillion oil paint spreading over the entire shirt, fanning out from the two epicenters. She was thinking, well at least it is not pulsatile, indicating it had not overtly hit an artery. She tried to keep running but everything was getting fuzzy and dark. She stumbled and fell. She kept trying to keep going, crawling on the beach. She tried to stand up and fell back onto the shore. She felt disoriented and could no longer tell where the men were. If they were still following her or had gone. She could feel the soft waves gently roll over her legs. The pain was lessening. It was becoming dull and her thoughts felt as though they were echoing in her head. She knew the numbing of the pain was an ominous sign. She was bleeding out. She was willing her body to move but her limbs felt like lead and she felt so tired, her energy was now directed to breathe, every breath needed to be coaxed out and then recoil in again. She was becoming part of the waves. Gentle and soothing. She suddenly felt light and agile. No pain at all. She was not struggling to breathe. She was not aware of breathing. The colors were brighter and more vivid than she had ever seen, like the most iridescent and beautiful rainbow one could imagine, they had the appearance of being pure translucent pigment. She could see lightning in the distance which illuminated the entire sky. The peace and magnificence would have been more than her earthly body could bear. She could not see any gunshot injuries on her body. She was clothed in a robe of shimmering white which seemed to contain all colors which coalesced as part of the vibrant white. Suddenly she felt ashamed to be in this garment which represented purity. She knew the darkness in her heart and started to weep.

In the distance she could see a man in a glorious white and gold robe with many crowns and with eyes like fire. His skin was radiant and would have been too bright for her eyes to see in the natural, but for the grace of her current disposition. His eyes contained the greatest gentleness and love she had ever witnessed or even thought possible. He seemed to know everything about her and love her still. She was afraid but enveloped in the greatest peace at the same time. All she could do was look upon Him, the one that was slain, the nail holes still present in His hands and feet with blood that seemed to have a life of its own, coming down in rivulets from his wounds and then dissipating into the atmosphere- resulting in a luminous mist of purpose. He looked deep into her soul.

"Emily," he called with a voice which sounded soft and roared like the sea at the same time. His words came from Him and were also visible as a funnel cloud coming from His mouth. It caused changes in the colors all around and the golden light would grow brighter when he spoke. His voice was vast.

Emily immediately knew all that He wanted to convey. "Jesus," she whispered.

"I am He."

"I am sorry about how I have lived my life," Emily blurted out as any infraction was burning into her spirit.

"I know."

"Why did you leave me? I have been so alone. I have wanted you, Lord. I have been in so much pain. Why?"

"My beloved. I was there.. I have held you many times. I have protected you. I have appeared to you in many forms and I have sent my messengers to guide you. You only needed to open your eyes. And your heart." " Why did you take Luke from me!" " MY child, there are things that you are not meant to understand right now, they are related to another's journey."

Immediately Emily had recalled all of the times He protected her and her children. That they weren't home when the house was broken in to, the man at the gas station with Maggie, Emily recognized him as an angel and that he had prevented her from getting into an accident that day, angels and his people, guiding her back to her mother and to Him. The times day in and day out that she had seen angels and interventions on her behalf. She knew all of these things in an instant. She began to weep so hard she thought her heart would shatter.

"I am sorry for my hardness of heart and my blindness. Help me Lord."

"Emily, I love you and I have already paid the price. You are redeemed" She noticed the nail wounds in his hands becoming more vivid. "I am with you always. I am the living water, I give life and quench your thirst. The thirst in your soul and spirit. I have called you by name." He held her in his lap for what seemed an eternity and an instant. She was a little child in her father's arms. She knew that He was the essence of all things. She thought her heart was going to explode with this knowledge. "Emily, take care of those I have entrusted to you and love them with the Father's heart. My love will never fail you and I will never leave you. You will have hardship as I have had hardships, but you will never do this alone. Do not seek what the world seeks and follow me as you are mine. You will then receive the crown of the faithful. Go and do all that I have asked you to do and you will come to me one day and live with me in paradise. This is the journey, my precious child. The journey to the light." He looked at her with the purest love and tenderness. "You need to go back and complete your path."

Before she could ask Him anything further, she could see the inside of the stabilization room and her body on the table. It looked so small and broken. The blood-stained shirt cut and on the floor. The paddles on her chest and numerous cannulas in her veins with spent vials on the cart. The medical staff working frantically with blood-stained scrubs. The valiant battle fought.

Emily was reluctant to go back into her body as she would again feel the weakness of her own mortality and she knew the pain that lay ahead in that body. The thought of her beautiful children pulled her into the lifeless body. Once back in her flesh, she immediately felt the excruciating pain. One of the doctors looked over at the nurse who was next to the crash cart.

"I am going to call it, what time is it?" At the same time as he was uttering these words, the flatline of the ECG voltage made a blip and then another and another. The electrical charges morphed into a robust QRS complex with normal T waves and then into a reassuring sinus rhythm. The battle won, this time.

Emily drifted in and out of consciousness but with a sense of peace and knowing that they would be okay. She was transported into the OR and then into the intensive care unit and within a few days was able to be transferred to the floor.

"Where are Oliver and Rachel?" were the first words out of her mouth. She was shouting this mantra when the nurse came in and came back a few minutes later with Bea. "Mom where are Oliver and Rachel? Are they okay? Please Jesus, let them be okay!"

"Emily, they're fine. They are with Noah. He just left with them to take them to the cafeteria for some dinner. Honey, we have all been here. Noah has taken such good care of those little children. He has also been so worried about you. We have all been praying over you and in the lobby and anywhere they would let us. My bible study has been praying non-stop for you."

"What happened to those men?" Everything started coming back to Emily.

"They were arrested not far from where you were found, one of them was killed. Oliver called nine-one-one and the police traced the call. Oliver also called Noah. I don't know how he got the number."

Emily remembered she had Noah in her contacts and Oliver knew the letters of Noah's name. She was impressed with his quick thinking. "Noah called me and I came back the next morning. He had the kids at his house overnight and hasn't left their sides. How are you, Emily? Are you in a lot of pain?"

"No, only a little." Emily smiled to hide her wincing from the reminder of her discomfort. She pressed the PCA button to administer more pain medication. "I just want to see my babies. Did they see what happened?" said Emily fearfully.

"No, they went to the house as you instructed. Some other people found you on the beach before the police had got there. Noah told them that you were okay and that they needed to hide under their bed until he got there. He called Orleen but he beat her to the house."

Everything was swimming in Emily's mind, how Noah had taken care of Oliver and Rachel and that they had been spared seeing the brutality. She had never been more grateful to anyone in her life. Maybe he was an angel. She remembered the beauty and majesty of Jesus and the love that seemed infinite. She continued to drift in and out of consciousness. A blessing to spare her from the pain.

She was awakened by the hushed voices of Oliver and Rachel. "Shh, Mommy is very tired," said Oliver trying to sound older and responsible.

"I want Mommy," cried Rachel.

"Oh, my sweet girl come to Mommy." Noah picked Rachel up and held her face close to Emily's face so she could kiss her. Emily tried to hold her but the pain from the wounds caused her to gasp slightly. Emily had become aware of the full impact of her injuries. She noticed a chest drain which was draining blood-tinged serous fluid. She also had an abdominal wound, which was more superficial. She would ask to look at her chart when her team came round and her brain cleared. "Oliver, you are so brave and smart. Thank you for taking such good care of Rachel."

"And me," said Rachel.

"Yes, and you too" It is okay if you are scared or worried." Oliver looked up at Emily and then hugged her. Emily was in pain but did not want to move for fear that he would feel rejection.

"I love you, Mommy."

"I love you too." Emily knew that his trauma most likely was not over. She would keep a careful watch. Emily looked up at Noah. He was holding Rachel's hand. She was trying to pull him around the room to find the card that she and Oliver had made for Emily.

"Here it is Mommy," Rachel said looking incredibly pleased with herself.

"Thank you, baby. It is the best card ever." The card was colorful with some scribbles and a stick figure in bed.

Emily would treasure this card forever. Bea offered to take the kids to see the fish tank in the hallway by the nurses' station. They both eagerly followed Bea out of the room. Emily looked up at Noah.

"Thank you for all that you have done for Oliver and Rachel."

He seemed a little embarrassed and looked away briefly. "Emily, I am so sorry that this happened to you. I love you." It was Emily's turn to look away. "It's okay Emily. I don't expect you to say anything. I just wanted to say it. I know it has only been a short time, but I felt connected to you from the first day I met you on the boat."

"Thanks again for taking care of my children. They clearly like you and trust you." Emily tried to push down her fear with the last statement. Noah gently touched her face. Emily knew that it must be swollen and bruised, but she could not see this in his eyes.

"I will be here when you need me." She was again mesmerized by the light dancing in his eyes. The stellate pattern. Maybe one day she would trust him too. Emily heard Bea and the children in the corridor. The enthusiastic steps and boisterous voices. Her family. Emily could tell that Oliver and Rachel were getting restless in the confines of the hospital so she would need to send them home with Bea, but she had to fight her need for their physical presence. She would talk to the team to see if she could expedite her discharge.

Overall, she was amazingly fortunate, the bullets managed to miss major blood vessels and her lung was healing. Her abdominal wound was clean and healing remarkably well. They would remove the chest drain as there was minimal drainage. Emily had placed and removed many chest drains in her training. She knew the drill, but it felt odd and vulnerable being on the other end of the procedure. Emily gave herself a bolus of narcotic before the procedure — which started with the dressing removal and the cleaning of the area — Emily could feel the cold betadine on her back. The suture holding the drain was snipped. Emily assumed there was a purse-string suture to pull tight once the drain was removed. Emily waited for the instruction to cough when removing the drain. This was more for distraction versus the benefit from the cough. The suture was pulled tight but not too tight to close the wound. Knots were tied and the excess suture was trimmed. This whole procedure was fairly slick and uncomplicated. The resident seemed pleased with himself for the skilled removal of the drain. She would need a CXR and the sutures removed next week. But for now, she was free from the drain and one step closer to discharge. Her team consisted of an attending and a resident and two medical students. They were cordial and respectful. There also seemed no small amount of ghoulish fascination with the injuries and the association with the criminal netherworld. They asked questions related to the sequence of events that lead to her injuries as much as about the injuries themselves.

Emily divided her time up with the hospital routines and visits from her beloved Oliver and Rachel. She also charged her phone and left a long message for Amy and

Mrs Lundgren. Emily texted Amy long updates about her clinical situation and her work in the shelter. It felt good writing the events out, it helped her brain make sense out of the chaos. Amy had only responded with short messages of surprise and concern. It did not matter, the process of writing was cathartic in and of itself. Emily also spent time praying and reading the Bible. It seemed an exciting thing to do, not a chore. She wanted to know more about Jesus and felt the light of His presence in these times. She would talk to Him throughout the day which proffered peace to her heart. She felt a transformation taking place from the inside out. It was about relationship, not religion.

Agent Osborne had sent flowers from the department. He came to visit. His awkward demeaner was even more so when facing Emily in the aftermath of the attack. His eyes betrayed some of the guilt which comes with the territory of policing. Emily had never had any contact with the police and now it had become almost routine. "Emily, I am glad we had the chip in the phone so when your son called the local police it triggered a response from our field agents as well. Louis Cortel and Joey Marco have been persons of interest for a while, they both worked for Dupont. The drug trafficking from the Carolinas to northern states like Minnesota has been ramping up and caught attention nationally. Thanks for your part in this mess."

"I appreciate your help, but I didn't do anything except be in the wrong place at the wrong time and in the wrong relationship."

"Okay, well, I want to discuss a few more things once you're out of here and mended. Take care." With a final glance toward Emily, he left.

Chapter 23
New Life and Healing Old Wounds

Time travels slowly and swiftly at the same time, but not linear. It is like we will keep revisiting the same things until we are done with these lessons. We heal in layers, the scab forms on the outside and the layers develop below the surface. Others can only guess at the degree of healing that has taken place. We seem to be moving forward only to revisit the pain or failure over and over again, and eventually in a more distant and transient manner. The wound becomes more stable and resilient to shearing forces. We become stronger but we know we are vulnerable by the presence of the scars.

Out of the hospital Emily felt more robust by the day. Oliver and Rachel were happy to have her home again. It had only been a little over a week, but it felt eons ago that she had gone to the Waffle Place with her children. This is also a peculiarity of life, we can have routines and long time periods without a substantial change in our perspectives, but then our whole thinking can change in an instant. Completely outside of our efforts. Emily spent her days with Oliver and Rachel and with Noah, walking on the beach, exploring islands on the 'ark'. Evenings were shared with bedtime routines and conversations between Emily and Noah, enthralling one another with opinions and hopes and stories of their lives, often talking until dawn. Emily had arranged to return part-time to the shelter after a few weeks. She wanted to spend the time at home to ensure Oliver and Rachel were coping all right and not too traumatized by the recent events. They seemed to enjoy having Noah around and were playing as if nothing had happened. Emily was too savvy to think that they were completely unaffected. She would continue to hold them closely. Emily was slowly letting down her guard with Noah. She was praying in the morning while sitting on the front porch, as had become her new normal, and felt an overwhelming sense that she should go through the letters from Luke.

"No Lord, it is still too soon. I don't want to bring the pain back."

"Emily, it's time," was all she felt as a response. Her hands were trembling as she removed the letters from the bag. She would keep those letters for Oliver and Rachel sealed and to give them to them when they were older. She could smell their old lives on the envelopes, Luke's aftershave and then smell of his office. First, she looked at the letter to his mother, which contained beautiful prose and apologies about not being the son she wanted and not being strong enough to care for her in her last days. He also apologizes for his descent into opiate addiction.

I numbed my pain because I couldn't' deal with yours. I had needed more and more to make this go away. I bought the opiates when I could not syphon pills from your dwindling supply. I have been filled with self-loathing for this weakness and the shame led to more and more squalid lapses. I am truly sorry, mother.

Luke, how I wish I had known you, was all Emily could think. She carefully removed the letter addressed to her from the papers.

My dearest Emily,

Emily smiled, Luke had always been a little dramatic.

If you are reading this letter, I am sure that I must be gone in some way, either via incarceration or in death. I am sorry for the pain you must now be feeling. I have been watching you sleep, your beautiful face resting in peaceful bliss. Your intelligent and forthright manner are all components of the only woman I have ever, or will ever, love. I have adored you and have been amazed by you over the years. I have also feared that you would know me completely and realize the failure of your choice. I wanted to hold you and to make love to you as my wife and partner, but I could not in the past months due to the knowledge of my precarious existence. That I have been living on a knife's edge and I wanted to protect you as much as I could. I was also afraid that you would really see me and that this would be reflected back. I could not face this much shame. In my descent into opiate oblivion, I have lied and cheated and dealt with less savory characters to feed the thirst. I stole money from our family such was my desperation. I made even more disagreeable arrangements to return the funds. Abby was traveling along the same course of depravity, so we traveled together. My journey has been one of appeasement and regret. I longed for 'the road less traveled' but I never regretted you or our children. I am weak which has been highlighted more and more by your strength. Even though I know you must be in pain, you must be elevated by the fact that I have loved you so completely, even in my impotence. I never betrayed this love despite my betrayal of our vows. I know you will raise our children with love, strength, and nobility of character. My love for you will go on long after I have departed this earth.

> Till a' the seas gang dry, my dear,
> And the rocks melt wi' the sun;
> I will love thee still, my dear,
> While the sands o'life shall run. ….
> And fare the weel, my only luve…!
> - *Robbie Burns.*

I know my lovely Emily that your candid manner is not moved by the honeyed words of the classics. I am at a loss to find the words to help you understand my great and broken love for you. I am sorry that I could not be the husband that you deserved. I beg forgiveness and offer my heart complete. Luke.

Tears required that Emily read this letter over and over to finish it in its entirety. She wished that she could go back in time and release him from the burdens which he could not bear, to help him carry these weights. She wanted him to know how to bear the trials. This was something that she had only recently discovered. She prayed for peace and for Luke, although there is no biblical basis for this plea. It calmed her nerves if nothing else. She found comfort in the fact that the eyes of Jesus held so much love and that this love for Luke was far greater than her own. "My lovely Luke you too have had my heart, and I too am sorry," she whispered softly.

Emily had received cards from the shelter and a fruit basket. She wanted to go back but wanted to do more to help. She would need to figure out if she could ever return to complete her residency. The hospital in Myrtle Beach was also part of the University of South Carolina and had a med-peds residency. Emily felt too tired to delve into this process right now. She just wanted to return to their new-found routines and recreate the stability of the past few months. Bea was kind and getting closer with Emily and Oliver and Rachel every day. Things were starting to settle again. Emily had even joined the bible study. Right now, she needed to plan Rachel's birthday. She also needed to get the promised dog as both children were becoming impatient in their waiting.

They had gone back to the beach where the evidence of the grisly event had been erased by the sea. The sea bringing rebirth. Emily felt uneasy heading down to the beach that first time, but Oliver and Rachel seemed to be oblivious to her internal angst. Noah saw them most days and would often come down to the beach with them. They seemed like a family. Emily loved gazing into his stellate eyes and then looking at the sea. She told him about her experience when she had been shot and how it changed her. The tender forgiveness of Jesus and His wisdom. Her spirit remembered Jesus' eyes and that He was also 'living water'. She instantly understood her attraction to the water. It was life giving, cleansing and symbolic of the Lord. His eyes also reflected His endless love and mercy. Eyes truly were 'the windows of the soul'.

Chapter 24
The New Journey

Rachel's birthday barbecue was exactly what she had wanted. Some of the regulars at the shelter had come and the bible study group, of which Emily was a full member. Neighbor children and, of course, Noah. Emily had help with Bea in planning and executing the party. Emily ordered the cake. A multicolored unicorn. Rachel played games and loved being the center of attention for the celebration. She opened her presents and cried, "This is my best day ever." Noah helped with the grilling and, overall, the day had been a success.

Once the clean-up was done, and both children tucked into bed, Emily and Noah sat on the porch swing together. He put his arm around her shoulder and kissed her gently on her cheek and then deeply on her lips. She still felt tingling all over her body when he touched her.

"Emily, I love you and I love Oliver and Rachel. I want us to be a family full time. I know this is soon and you have all been through so much, but I need to say this." Noah turned her face towards him. "Will you be my wife?" He handed her small jewelers' box. She opened it and inside was an exquisite marquis diamond set in antique white gold.

"It's beautiful, I don't know what to say."

"Say yes," he smiled his most charming smile. "The ring had been my mother's."

"I love you too, Noah." She hesitated and said, "I just need a little time."

She handed back the box, but he put his hand over hers and said, "Hold on to this while you're making up your mind." He kissed her again, but with greater intensity. With that he left.

In the morning both children were up early in anticipation of going to a local 'olden reliever' breeder. Emily got them fruit and yogurt and then drove over the bridge and onto South Carolina proper. The home was on a sprawled-out ranch. Oliver and Rachel could hardly contain themselves when they arrived, trying to get out of their car seats before the car had stopped. A tall woman in a plaid shirt and faded jeans met them. Her jeans had various stains and a thin coat of dust.

"Hi, I'm Carol," she said cheerfully as she extended her hand. "I take it that you're Emily and these two are the prospective puppy owners."

Both children excitedly said, "Yes." She guided them over to the barn where there were five rambunctious puppies. A couple were sandy in color and three were creamy white. Rachel squealed in excitement as she ran toward one of the cream-colored puppies. She picked him up and snuggled him to her nose.

"Look, Ollie and this puppy." Oliver picked up a few of the other puppies and then settled on the puppy that Rachel had in her lap.

Carol came over and said, "This is a good choice. He has a lot of energy but also loves to be held. Perfect for a home with children."

Emily brought out of the car the carrier which contained a few toys. "What are we going to call him?" said Oliver looking up at Emily.

"What would you guys like to call him?"

"I want to call him Sunflower," said Rachel.

Oliver turned up his nose and said, "We can't call a boy dog called Sunflower."

"What about, Rubble?" Rachel reluctantly agreed.

Emily picked up the dog carrier, after signing the paperwork and writing a check for Rubble, and they were off.

Work had restarted and evenings were drawing in. In the mornings, she had developed a habit of getting up and walking down the long driveway to the mailbox and then looking over the mail with her coffee on the porch. She completed this with her prayers and reading of the Word. Today was no different. She had grabbed the mail from the rusty mailbox and had made her coffee in the mug that Rachel had picked out for her and sat down on one of the wicker chairs. Picking through the mail, she noticed a letter from Myrtle Beach Hospital. She assumed it was a bill from the previous month's hospital stay. She opened the envelope and it started out with:

Congratulations Doctor Warrington on your acceptance to the med-peds program at Myrtle Beach.

She looked and read it again, and then again. They had accepted her previous training and she would only do two months to complete her residency. She called the program as she thought it must be some mistake. The program director had gone over her application and reported references from Drs Meyer, Fishman and Roberts in supporting her application. She had been most highly regarded. The only person who would have filled out her application was Amy. Emily called her immediately and Amy quickly admitted to the deed.

"Thank you so much Amy, I don't know how to repay you."

"Emily, there you go again. You are my friend and there is nothing to repay. I would like somewhere warm to stay over Christmas though."

"Any time Amy."

"Mrs Lungren came back to Minnesota after Abby died. She couldn't see staying in North Carolina without Abby. Oh, and she said that Abby had several small brown parcels in her apartment. She thinks she got them from your house before she left the state. Before your house was set alight. The word is, that they were opiates."

"Wow," was all Emily could muster. Her mind racing with processing all of the emotionally laden information.

"I am glad that your life is quieter now and that Oliver and Rachel are happy. Now tell me about the gorgeous guy in the picture you sent."

Emily immediately thought about Noah. "Noah is a captain of a boat who does tours and some fishing. He used to be a corporate lawyer in DC, but gave it up. His family is from here, which eventually pulled him back to his roots. He has been amazing to the kids and to me. I think I am falling in love with him."

The last part startled both of them.

"So what are you going to do about it?" said Amy with her typical pragmatism.

"I don't know. I am just getting through each day. Emily deliberately omitted the part about the marriage proposal. But wasn't certain as to why. How are you, Amy? How is your divorce and job hunting?"

"I have pretty much landed on my feet. The divorce has gone through, which has been a relief for the most part. I managed to get a hospitalist job at Regions Hospital. I am starting to pay off my loans. So I guess I am doing okay as a grown up."

"Amy, you know that we are your family, right?"

"I know. But it is still good to hear, as my bio family is kind of messed up."

Emily ended the call and just sat frozen reflecting over the past year. Processing and more processing. You really never know what the future holds, what is solid and what is an illusion. She felt stronger and more tentative as a result. She was learning to live in the moment and to be thankful with things as they were. The Lord, Rachel, Oliver, Bea, Noah and Amy: her family. Their lives inextricably linked. This was their journey, despite what hardships lay ahead. And it was radiant.

The End